Telemakos

"Stand still, bow properly, and be introduced," said Kidane. "Princess Goewin, this is Telemakos Meder. He is the issue of my daughter Turunesh and our former British ambassador, as you may guess. He takes his second name from his father: Ras Meder, Prince Meder, is how Medraut's son thinks of him." He pushed the child forward.

"Telemakos, this is the Princess Goewin, who arrived in the city this morning. She is daughter to Artos the dragon, the high king of Britain. She will be the queen of her own country when she goes home, though she is dressed humbly enough for traveling; and she also happens to be your aunt. You must treat her with appropriate respect."

Telemakos bowed low at my feet, on his knees, with his forehead just touching the ground. His movements were all light and quick and efficient. No one had ever bent before me so submissively.

"Welcome, lady, welcome to Aksum," Telemakos said demurely. "I am your servant."

"Look up," I commanded him, because I was wild to see his eyes again. "Look at my face a moment."

He raised his head. His eyes were blue, such a deep familiar blue, like slate or smoke. His skin was the color of ale or cider, his front teeth were missing, he was very little; but by heaven, he looked like Medraut.

FIREBIRD
WHERE FANTASY TAKES FLIGHT™

A Coalition of Lions

ELIZABETH E. WEIN

FIREBIRD

AN IMPRINT OF PENGUIN GROUP (USA) INC.

FIREBIRD

Published by Penguin Group

Penguin Group (USA) Inc.,

345 Hudson Street, New York, New York 10014, U.S.A.

Penguin Books Ltd, 80 Strand, London WC2R ORL, England

Penguin Books Australia Ltd, 250 Camberwell Road, Camberwell, Victoria 3124, Australia

Penguin Books Canada Ltd, 10 Alcorn Avenue, Toronto, Ontario, Canada M4V 3B2

Penguin Books (N.Z.) Ltd, 182-190 Wairau Road, Auckland 10, New Zealand

First published in the United States of America by Viking,
a division of Penguin Putnam Books for Young Readers, 2003
Published by Firebird, an imprint of Penguin Group (USA) Inc., 2004

"Book I: Athena Inspires the Prince," from *The Odyssey* by Homer, translated
by Robert Fagles, copyright © Robert Fagles, 1996. Used with permission
of Viking Penguin, a division of Penguin Group (USA) Inc.

1 3 5 7 9 10 8 6 4 2

THE LIBRARY OF CONGRESS HAS CATALOGED THE VIKING EDITION AS FOLLOWS:

Wein, Elizabeth.

Coalition of lions / Elizabeth Wein.

p. cm.

Summary: After the death of Artos, High King of Britain, and his sons,
his daughter Princess Goewin journeys to Aksum to meet Constantine,
her intended husband, but finds the country in political turmoil.

ISBN: 0-670-03618-8 (hc)

[1. Princesses—Fiction. 2. Arthur, King—Fiction. 3. Aksum (Kingdom)—Fiction.
4. Mordred (Legendary character)—Fiction.] I. Title.

PZ7.W4355 Go 2003 [Fic]—dc21 2002015552

Puffin ISBN 0-14-240129-3

Printed in the United States of America

FOR TIM,

with all my love, a gift of paper

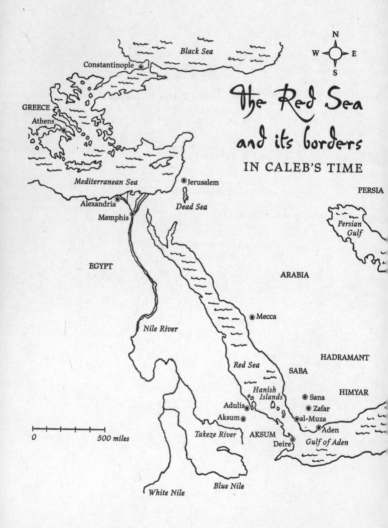

The Red Sea and its borders IN CALEB'S TIME

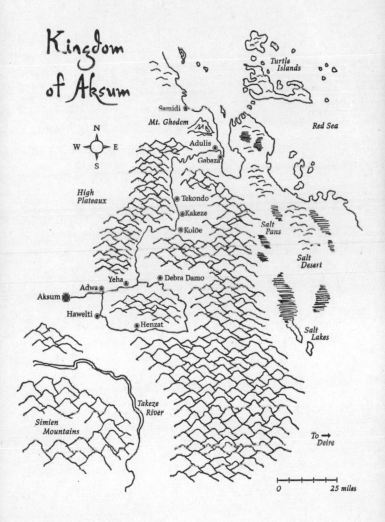

Contents

✧

PART III: FLIGHT

PART IV: FORGIVENESS

A Coalition of Lions

Prologue

THE EMPEROR'S COUNSELOR stopped reading. He looked up and spoke the next lines off by heart. "'Love is strong as death,'" Kidane said. "'Jealousy is cruel as the grave.'" He had been reading aloud from the Song of Songs. "'Many waters cannot quench love, neither can floods drown it. If a man offered for love all the wealth of his house, it would be utterly scorned.'"

Kidane rolled the scrolls shut. Turunesh had set a pot of water to boil over the ceremonial brazier, and she and her father were about to drink one last ritual cup of coffee with their young British guest. Tomorrow Medraut's embassy in African Aksum would end, and he would begin his long journey, four thousand miles across the world, back to his father's kingdom in Britain.

"We will miss you deeply, Medraut," Kidane said. "Our home has become your home. You are not the inexperienced boy you were when you arrived. You have earned your Aksumite name, Ras Meder, Prince Meder, lord of the land. We will miss you more than I can say."

The garden court was dark but for the hanging lamps. Turunesh's doves and parrots were asleep. The white, alcoved walls of the enclosure were full of shadows; lamplight rippled in the black waters of the granite fish pool. Kidane's face was difficult for Medraut to see, for the light fell over his shoulder, but the counselor's voice was warm and filled with sadness as he spoke.

Medraut knelt and lifted his host's hands from the book to kiss them lightly. "And I will miss you," he replied in Ethiopic, the language he had spoken for nearly three years and which he took pride in being able to read and write. "You are right: Aksum has made me. I am forever in your debt. I leave you with nothing of myself, and you and your daughter have given of your gifts and affection generously and generously."

He turned toward Turunesh, but she sat with her head bent, her attention fixed on the roasting coffee. Medraut quickly looked away from her. Lizards leaped and murdered moths in the thatched awning over their heads. The night air was full of the bitter fragrance of coffee, but also smelled faintly of frankincense, as the scent blew down from the plantation on the neighboring hillside.

Medraut did not easily speak of himself, and he had never heard any Aksumite make painful confessions about his or her emotional state. But he wanted to explain himself a little, on this last night in the house of the dark, regal girl he had come to love.

"I had no sense of my own worth when I arrived in Aksum," Medraut said in a low voice. "Since their birth I have lived in envy of my small half-brother, Lleu, and Goewin, his twin sister. But Aksum has made me. I have become myself here. Why should I envy anyone? If Hector and Priamos can serve their uncle the emperor so selflessly, after a childhood of exile and imprisonment, then so may I serve my own king."

Turunesh spoke chidingly as she laid out the earthen cups. "You let a deal of nonsense pass your lips, Medraut son of Artos. You know the sequestering of lesser princes is traditional, and Caleb never planned to keep his nephews at Debra Damo forever. You can be sure your father has a plan for you, as well. Will you follow him as high king?"

"Not while Lleu lives. Lleu is the queen's son, I am not. I will serve as Britain's regent, perhaps, or its steward."

"There is no greater service on this earth than stewardship," said Kidane. "A true king is his people's steward; their lives, and their faith, are in his hands."

Turunesh began to pour the coffee, still berating Medraut. "And that you would call the hermitage at Debra Damo a prison, after your visit there with the emperor Caleb himself as your guide! You were aglow with holiness and delight on your return."

"You speak perfect truth, as ever," Medraut admitted, glowing again with the memory of that visit: the rare, clear air of the amba plateau, the fantastically carved and gilded church there, the reservoirs hewn from the living rock, the twisted strap of leather rope that was the only way up the cliff. He thought of the emperor Caleb's companionship, of his trust and honor.

"Now I have become—"

He hesitated, and Turunesh murmured without looking up from her deft hands: "Warrior, statesman, huntsman. Lion killer." She raised her head from the coffee at last, and smiled, though she did not meet his eyes. No Aksumite had ever met his eyes. They would have considered it a great insolence to do so; he was the eldest son of Britain's high king.

"And Christian," Turunesh added, smiling still. "You were baptized here. What will Artos your father say to that?"

"He'll say, Africa is always producing something new."

They all three laughed together.

Kidane held out his hand again to Medraut. "Get off your knees, you sentimental boy," he said.

Medraut took his seat, embarrassed. Turunesh handed him his coffee, bitter and black. He cupped the hot beaker between his hands, breathing in the strong steam.

"I've put a great dose of honey in it," Turunesh said, "to sweeten it for you. I know you don't really like it."

"I like the smell."

"You have to share a cup with us, this last night before you go."

"I know." Medraut sighed again. "If the kingship of Britain were offered to me tomorrow, I would throw it away for the promise that I will share another cup of coffee with you before I die."

"Don't," Turunesh said softly. "You will set me to weeping."

Medraut sipped gingerly at the steaming black liquor.

"Sweet enough?" she inquired.

"'Out of the strong came something sweet,'" he murmured, quoting Samson's riddle of bees and honey in the carcass of the slain lion.

"Lion killer," Turunesh murmured in answer, teasing. "What did you mean, you have left us with nothing of yourself? I shall never pass your lion skin hanging in the reception hall without thinking of you."

They drank the coffee. The lamps in the standards that stood about the garden court began to burn low. Turunesh lifted one down.

"'Return, return,'" she whispered to the lamp, as though she were weaving an incantation. The flame burned steadily, pale white-gold and smoky blue, the color of Medraut's hair and eyes. "'Return, return.'"

Her father could not have heard her, but Medraut could. Turunesh whispered the words Kidane had read aloud earlier from the Song of Songs. "'Return, return, that we may look upon you.'"

She held the lamp high and turned to face the young British ambassador.

"Come, Medraut," she said aloud. "I'll light you to your room."

PART
I

SANCTUARY

CHAPTER ONE

❖

Naming the Animals

SIX YEARS AFTER Medraut returned to Britain, and a bare season after he and my twin brother Lleu nearly killed each other over which of them should be the high king's heir, our father's estate at Camlan was destroyed in a battle that began by accident.

Camlan shattered Medraut. He began the battle: he drew his sword to kill an adder at my father's heel, and the host mustered by Cynric of the West Saxons fell on our own soldiers at the flash of light on metal. When sickness attacked the nearby village of Elder Field in the battle's wake, and my mother waited on the stricken without stint until she, too, was killed by the fever, Medraut blamed himself for not relieving her. Then Medraut killed our father. Artos asked it of him, rather than lie waiting to die of his battle wounds. Before that final damning act of courage and mercy, Medraut had spent a day and most of a night limping on a broken knee through the frozen, bloody fields around Camlan, searching for Lleu. It was not three months since Lleu had kissed and forgiven him his last winter's betrayal. Medraut would have given his own life to spare our brother's. All he found of my twin after Camlan was the golden circlet Lleu had worn.

Then Medraut disappeared. He lost himself in the caves at Elder Field, where we buried my parents and cousins. When I discovered he was gone, I felt my way in panic down the tunnel that led beyond the crypt, beyond the reach of the little light burning at my father's head, until I was afraid to go any farther. I stood there, calling and calling my elder brother, until I had to shut up because I suddenly so hated the sound of my own voice in that deep, quiet dark.

I and my father's soldiers searched and waited for Medraut for a month. But then came the rumor that the Saxon lord Cynric had offered a bounty for me, and my father's treacherous sister Morgause announced she would pay my weight in silver for proof that I was dead. I knew she meant it. I had seen the scars she left on Medraut, and he and I had spent half of the last summer battling to keep her from poisoning Lleu. Now only I stood between my aunt and her lost sovereignty. I panicked like a hunted doe. In fear and grief I turned my back on my own kingdom, with all the forethought and resolution of a gazelle flying before a crouching lioness.

I fled first to Father's capital in Deva. In the garrison there waited confirmation of Cynric's bride price; as his messenger he sent me Priamos Anbessa, my father's African envoy.

Priamos, too, had sought for Lleu after Camlan, and had found
him torn with spear and ax, and was made prisoner with him.
He sat awake with Lleu through the night before Lleu died.
Cynric sent Priamos back to me bearing the news of my brother's death, and the offer of Cynric's protection and dowry if I
agreed to marry one of his grandsons.

Seriously, quietly, my father's dark ambassador from the
Red Sea kingdom of Aksum delivered me his message from
the Saxon lord, then offered me the sanctuary of his own
empire.

As far back as I can remember there had always been an
Aksumite ambassador in my father's court, an aloof, reserved
young man with skin the color of peat and eyes that never met
your own. They saw to it that we received ivory and papyrus,
salt and spices and emeralds from the lands of the Red Sea,
and that my father sent their king tin and silver and wool
in fair exchange. I knew I could trust Priamos's offer. My cousin Constantine had long served in Aksum as our own ambassador there, in Medraut's place. My father had named
Constantine as my future husband, and as his heir after my
brothers. If I traveled to Aksum I could call Constantine
home myself. I let Priamos lead me.

Three months later I sat in the New Palace in the imperi-
al city of Aksum, at the edge of the big fountain in the Golden
Court, seeking sanctuary, and waiting an audience with
Constantine.

It was Constantine who was making me wait. I found, on

my arrival, that my cousin had somehow so ingratiated himself with the Aksumite emperor that Caleb had abdicated in Constantine's favor. Constantine was no longer Britain's ambassador to Aksum; he was now viceroy of Aksum. So although half my father's soldiers had got in the habit of calling me queen of Britain since the high king's death, I had to sit in the Golden Court and wait for my cousin to grant me an audience.

The Golden Court echoed with the sound of running water and the chattering of colobus monkeys. The monkeys were a strange and beautiful highland breed, with flowing white tails and long fur that draped about their shoulders in a black-and-white cape. They crouched on the floor and in the potted palm trees, tethered by slender gold chains fixed in the sides of the fountains. The sound of the water was soothing; the chattering of the monkeys was not. They shook their chains and screamed whenever anyone walked through the hall.

"They make me think of that boy we saw in Septem, when you made us change ships a day early," I said to Priamos, sitting at my right hand. "Do you remember the child servant on the yacht berthed next to ours, that they led on board by his bound wrists?"

"Except these creatures strain against their bonds," Priamos answered, "and that boy did not."

"I would."

Priamos touched the side of my hand, briefly, as he had done at the time. "You would." His dark, narrow face seemed all sharpness and severity behind his pointed black beard, but I knew that his serious frown hid humor and kindness. He was only a little older than I. "I would, too, Princess."

"And they make me think of my aunt." But everything made me think of Morgause. "She kept a menagerie of exotic creatures, all bound and caged."

At my left, Kidane, the counselor who had once been Medraut's host, held out his hands in a gesture of peace and welcome. "Be at ease, Princess Goewin," he said. "A death sentence is a chilling burden, and must be especially so for one who is scarcely past girlhood. How unfortunate that a thing so harmless as a pet monkey should remind you of your flight. Try to be at ease. You are safe, here, for a time."

All the events of the cold, sad spring just past had led me to this meeting with Constantine, yet the only thing I could think of was my aunt. And what I kept thinking about was not the vicious cruelty she had inflicted on my brothers, nor the harm she wished on me, but with what desperation she battled the men around her who sought to keep her power for their own, who strove to hold her helpless.

There was a sudden commotion among the monkeys, as four or five of them scampered toward a single point on the other side of the big fountain. The rest stretched out at the limit of their gold chains, screeching with jealous longing. A small person of about six years stood camouflaged among the palms, holding out his hands to the monkeys. In this land of dark-skinned people, his hair was a shocking white-gold blaze, nearly as pale as that of an albino. I stared at him and bit my lip, my heart twisting within me. He had my elder brother's hair.

Kidane stood up and turned around, gazing toward the clustering monkeys.

"Oh, that wretched child," he said. "He has been told not to feed these creatures." Kidane strode around the fountain. "Telemakos! Give me that. Come away now, or I will see to it you do not leave the house for a week."

Kidane came back to us, with a branch of dates in one hand and the child led cruelly by the ear in the other. The small boy bore this abuse stoically, his lips pressed together in a tight, thin line, his eyes narrowed in contained anger.

"I thought you were in council all this week, Grandfather," he protested. "No one else minds if I feed them."

"They mind the havoc it creates." Kidane released the child's ear and gripped him by the shoulder, as if he expected his grandson to try to slip away from him suddenly.

The boy was neatly slender, foxlike in his movements. His skin was the deep gold-brown of baked bread or roasted wheat. And his hair, his hair: it was thick as carded wool and white as sea foam, like a bundle of bleached raw silk. It was Medraut's hair.

Kidane spoke quietly and severely to him in Latin: "*How unseemly!* Questioning me before a guest, and she the princess of Britain! Speak Latin so that the princess can understand."

The child ducked his head in apology. He spoke in Latin,

but only to repeat what he had said in Ethiopic: "Why are you not in council, Grandfather?"

"The bala heg does not meet until this afternoon. You are an embarrassment," said Kidane. "Stand still, bow properly, and be introduced. Princess Goewin, this is Telemakos Meder. He is the issue of my daughter Turunesh and our former British ambassador, as you may guess. He takes his second name from his father: Ras Meder, Prince Meder, is how Medraut's son thinks of him." He pushed the child forward.

"Telemakos, this is the Princess Goewin, who arrived in the city this morning. She is daughter to Artos the dragon, the high king of Britain. She will be the queen of her own country when she goes home, though she is dressed humbly enough for traveling; and she also happens to be your aunt. You must treat her with appropriate respect."

Telemakos bowed low at my feet, on his knees, with his forehead just touching the ground. His movements were all light and quick and efficient. No one had ever bent before me so submissively.

"Welcome, lady, welcome to Aksum," Telemakos said demurely. "I am your servant."

"Look up," I commanded him, because I was wild to see his eyes again. "Look at my face a moment."

He raised his head. His eyes were blue, such a deep familiar blue, like slate or smoke. His skin was the color of ale or cider, his front teeth were missing, he was very little; but by heaven, he looked like Medraut.

He asked me abruptly, "Why are you my aunt?"

"I am your father's sister," I answered.

"Oh," Telemakos said, and looked me up and down before lowering his eyes again, still on his knees. He glanced at his grandfather. "You said she is a princess."

"Your father was a prince. We have told you that. Ras Priamos is a prince, also," Kidane hinted.

Telemakos lowered his head again. It was not so deep a bow as he had made to me; but I sensed that there was more sincerity, or at any rate more intensity, in this reverence. "Peace to you, Ras Priamos," he said. "I remember you."

"You cannot be old enough to remember me," said Priamos. He had left Aksum nearly a year ago.

"I do remember you. I remember the parade, after the war in Himyar, when you led your beaten warriors through the cathedral square."

Telemakos spoke with deep and unfeigned devotion.

"I was little, but I won't ever forget, my lord. Your uncle the emperor called you anbessa, his lion. Your warriors stood so silent, holding their spears upside down, their clothes all bloody. And you were naked to the waist to show how sorry you were. The emperor took your sword back, and hit your shoulders and face with its flat side because you had lost the battle, but he called you lionheart."

Priamos went very still. I had seen him unhappy before: quiet and frowning when my father's estate was under attack, and choked with stoppered emotion when he had to tell me of Lleu's death; and quiet again, but acting with determined purpose to get me aboard a different ship, when he had suspected I was being tracked by a spy of Cynric's or my aunt's. Priamos was always quiet when he was disturbed. But I had never seen him this still. His brow was so heavy that he always seemed to scowl, even when he was calm, and it could have meant nothing; except he was so still.

I had known of his army's defeat, but he had kept his personal failure closely guarded. I looked away, at the fountain, at the chattering monkeys, so I should not seem to notice the shameful scars on his soul stripped bare like this.

Priamos said at last, "My uncle only called me by my name."

"Lionheart," Telemakos insisted. "Priamos Anbessa, he called you."

"We are all called Anbessa, I and my brothers and sisters. My father's name was Anbessa, and we are called Anbessa after him, as you are called Meder."

"Lion—"

Kidane cleared his throat ominously. Telemakos swallowed, and contained himself. He managed to say, "Welcome, most noble prince, welcome to your homeland."

"Get off your knees," Priamos said gently.

Telemakos moved to sit at my feet, and winningly clasped one of my hands between his own small, brown ones. "Stay with us, Princess Goewin," he said. He said to me: "'Greetings, stranger! Here in our house you'll find a royal welcome. Have supper first, then tell us what you need.'" I stared down at his bowed head. He was reciting from Homer's *Odyssey*.

His grandfather did not recognize it. "That is the most polite string of words you have ever uttered," Kidane remarked.

Priamos burst into his rare, sweet and merry laughter, like a child. "What a gifted grandson you have!" he exclaimed. "The young charmer! He's quoting his namesake, Odysseus's son Telemakos. Greeting you with winged words, Princess! Those are Telemakos's first words to the goddess Athena."

"I know." I spoke softly.

"I meant it, though," Telemakos said, unabashed. "Will you stay in my grandfather's house in Aksum, Princess Goewin, and become my mother's friend, as your brother did?"

Kidane had already made me this offer, but coming from Telemakos it suddenly made my throat close up and my eyes swim. I had come four thousand miles, in fear of my life, hoping to find sanctuary among strangers; and instead here I was offered a home by my brother's son, as he sat at my feet clasping my hand in his, greeting me as a goddess.

"Thank you," I answered. "Yes, I would delight to stay in your house."

"That is all right, isn't it, Grandfather?"

"For the moment," Kidane told him. "The princess may decide to stay in the palace, after she meets the viceroy. She is to be married to Constantine."

"Today?"

Kidane laughed. "Not today. Next year, when they return

to Britain. The monsoon is beginning; they cannot travel until winter is over, and even then they may postpone their journey until the Red Sea winds blow in their favor. Now go away, if you are going to ask impertinent questions."

"I will be polite. Let me get my animals, and I will come and wait with you." Telemakos scrambled to his feet again.

"My Noah's Flood animals," he explained over his shoulder, in case any of us thought he might mean the colobus monkeys he had been illegally feeding.

Kidane settled by me, lowering himself onto the wide stone lip of the fountain as though his grandson's high spirits weighed too heavily on his shoulders for his body to endure. He laid the date branch at his side and smoothed flat the embroidered edges of his white robe. I asked quickly, under my breath, "Did Medraut know about Telemakos?"

"He did not. He left us many months before the child was born."

Telemakos returned with a canvas satchel slung over his shoulder. He knelt before me again and began to take a series of lovely wooden figurines from his bag; these he ranged across the floor at my feet.

Priamos said, "Look at those animals!"

Telemakos glanced up and gave a respectful nod. "Pass them up here," Priamos directed. "The princess has never seen creatures like these. You will have to teach her their names, so we can take her hunting when the rains end."

"I don't know the Latin," Telemakos said.

"Latin's no use to anyone," said Priamos. He had been trained as an interpreter. He was not boastful, but he was given to flaunting his gift for languages. He had spent the long hours aboard ship telling me stories in his native Ethiopic and in Greek, the common language of the Red Sea, that I might learn a little of his speech before arriving in his homeland. "Use Greek or Ethiopic."

Telemakos pressed the wooden animals into my hands: rhinoceros, leopard, ostrich, ibex.

"Do you like hunting, Princess Goewin?" Telemakos asked. "My mother rides in the hunt, but she does not shoot."

"I like hunting," I said.

"Do you shoot?"

"Yes."

"I am a terrible shot. I'm a good tracker, though."

Kidane laughed at him again. "You'd be lucky, boy. The gazelle of the Great Valley are a deal faster than those fat and lazy things the emperor keeps as pets. We'll take you along some day and see how close you get."

Telemakos lowered his gaze without argument, and I could see that he did as much stalking outside the palace walls as he did within them, only no one was supposed to know that. I thought to myself: His grandfather has no idea what this child's limits are.

Baboon, buffalo, elephant, oryx. Telemakos continued to hand me his procession of wooden animals. Priamos, relenting, did try to remember the Latin names for them, but even he did not know them all: zebra, giraffe.

"These are my favorite," Telemakos said: a lion and lioness.

"Leo," I said. "Llew, in my mother's native dialect."

Telemakos placed the lion on my open palm.

"That's why Father called my brother Lleu the young lion, sometimes," I said softly, "though his name really means the Bright One. Llew: leo: anbessa."

I held the wooden lion before me in my cupped hand. Its painted mane was black; its carved jaw was caught midsnarl, showing white teeth.

"Caleb had to wrestle a lion to prove he was strong enough to be emperor," Telemakos said.

"He had to catch it," Kidane corrected.

"His lions were tame. They ate from his hands."

"They were not tame," Priamos said quietly. "They were chained."

Telemakos took back his lion and put it on the floor in file beside its mate at the head of his pageant. He bent his head over the animals.

"They were tame," he insisted.

His clear voice softened with something like adoration. "Caleb let me touch them, before you took them to Britain. He let me stroke their manes, after I was presented to him last new year. Are they still in Britain?"

"They were destroyed when my father's estate was burned," I said. "I'm sorry, my love. There was a battle, and my parents and brothers were killed. That is why I came here."

"Oh." Telemakos tapped his wooden lions with the palm

of his hand, then closed the hand into a fist and laid it in his lap. He asked slowly, "Are all the high king's children killed, then?"

"All but I," I answered.

Telemakos held still, bent over his lions. If it dawned on him that I had just told him his father was dead, he did not draw attention to it. "You were lucky to get away," he said at last.

"I must go back," I told him.

CHAPTER II

Ella Amida

"PRINCESS GOEWIN. THE viceroy sends to tell you he is at your service."

The courtier who knelt before me was no older than I. He was dressed like Kidane, with a shamma overmantle and head cloth of closely woven linen, except that this young man's head cloth was banded with ribbons of silver mesh.

"This is Ityopis Anbessa," said Kidane, "another of the brothers lionheart."

"Please don't kneel," I repeated. His formality infected everyone. Kidane and Priamos were on their feet, and Telemakos knelt on both knees with his face in his hands. What a trial it must be, I thought, to be six and not quite royal, and to have to throw yourself on the floor whenever any adult walks into the room. Father had never demanded such ceremony of me or Lleu.

Ityopis stood up. The brothers lionheart faced each other.

"Hornbill!" Ityopis cried in delight, and they caught each other's shoulders and touched cheek to cheek. "I did not know you had been sent for!"

Priamos did not meet his brother's eyes. "I have not been sent for," he answered. "I came here as guide and translator for the princess, but no one sent for me."

"And you trusted him, Princess?" Ityopis was laughing. "'Have no trust in translators,' that is what our uncle the emperor Caleb would have told you. Though he had Abreha in mind when he said it, I think, not Priamos Hornbill."

"Abreha?" I asked.

"The self-styled king of Himyar," Kidane said. "The victorious pretender."

"He who won the battle against Ras Priamos," Telemakos supplied, the gap in his teeth making him whistle over Priamos's name.

"Abreha's title is not self-styled," Priamos said with his habitual scowl, though his voice was mild enough. "He was elected."

"Let's not talk of Himyar," Ityopis said quickly. "My fault for speaking Abreha's name. Our mother the queen of queens will have to call me Hornbill instead of you, Priamos. Has he explained why the queen of queens names him Hornbill, Princess—"

"Because I look like one," Priamos interrupted, his heavy brow lowered ferociously.

"Because his tongue will never be reined when he is nervous or excited, and lets slip a deal of nonsense that were better left unsaid."

I raised my own eyebrows. "Truly?"

"Has he not yet gone off his head with temper in your presence? Perhaps you have enspelled him, Princess—"

"Ityopis, keep hold of your own tongue or I will find someone to cut it out," Priamos interrupted hotly, and said to me, "Pay no heed to this lapdog of his mother. He has always been abominably disrespectful of all his elder brothers. Sits on the emperor's council and gets called dove, the peacemaker, by the emperor Caleb's elder sister, our mother Candake the queen of queens! What monstrous rot!"

Through all this exchange they had not let go of each other's shoulders.

"Tell me of my brothers, Peacemaker," Priamos said. "Have you word of Mikael?"

"He sits as ever on his cliff top at Debra Damo, reciting the tale of Daniel a hundred times a day."

"And Yared?"

"Sings. They say he is devising a way to write down his music. Perhaps Yared will be released from his sequestering when he is a little older, as you and I were," Ityopis said. "And as Hector was."

"And Abreha," said Telemakos.

His grandfather struck him. Not hard enough to call it cruel, but hard enough to hurt. Telemakos knelt again. His poor knees. He hid his face in his hands and said humbly, "I don't know what I did that time, Grandfather. I beg your pardon."

Kidane sighed.

"Ityopis has said we will not speak of Himyar anymore," Kidane said. "Don't just hear what people say: listen. If you listen to everything, and keep your mouth shut until someone asks you a question, you won't offend anyone. You'll hear more that way, as well, because you won't be sent off in disgrace. And, God willing, you'll learn to tell what's spoken appropriately, and what isn't.

"Listen," Kidane repeated.

"Yes," Telemakos said quietly. "Yes, sir."

And I, who had been listening carefully the whole time, realized that the pretender Abreha was also Priamos's brother.

Constantine sat in a room of black and green marble. He was surrounded by attendant courtiers, and had the ceremonial spear bearers of the Aksumite emperor, the negusa nagast, king of kings, at his back. One of the company, a boy of fourteen or fifteen years who wore a plain white cotton shamma and head cloth, watched me steadily and frankly, which was the first time anyone in Aksum had eyed me other than with oblique glances. And in truth I must have been a troubling sight: unadorned with gold or precious jewels, my hair plaited and pinned up simply in the way I had learned to care for it myself during my journey, my skirt patched and faded.

Constantine rose and came forward to greet me. He was not much taller than me, and close to my age, like Priamos.

His sandy hair was banded with an Aksumite head cloth; he wore a small pointed beard, also like Priamos. He took me by the hands and said, "Welcome, cousin, to the imperial city of the Aksumite peoples."

He spoke Latin, which meant that most there could not understand what he was saying. "My dear Goewin, you are still so very young!" he said. "How did you dare the journey from Britain? What can have brought you here? Could you not wait until next year for a husband?"

I could not return his smile. I answered stiffly in my limping Ethiopic, so that my words should not need to be translated or told twice. "I did not come seeking a husband. I came seeking the protection of the emperor Caleb, Ella Asbeha, who brought forth the dawn, my father's most powerful and influential ally."

"The emperor could not have made that offer himself," said Constantine. It was a bald statement of truth, lacking of sympathy or interest, and my dislike of him grew.

"He did not," I said patiently. "I had the invitation from Ras Priamos, the emperor Caleb's nephew and envoy. Priamos did not expect, and neither did I, to find his emperor's kingdom made handsel to a foreign princeling."

That insulted him, as it was meant to. Constantine stood pressing his lips together. Then for the first time he glanced at Priamos, who for months had been my most true and brave companion. "Priamos Anbessa," said Constantine softly, in Ethiopic also. "What are you doing in this city?"

The question took Priamos by surprise.

"Make a reply," said Constantine.

Priamos answered reasonably, his voice low, "I could not let the princess journey alone."

"You were sent to Britain for an appointment that should last no less than three years. You have acted in direct defiance of your king in coming here. Was there no gratitude in you for being entrusted with such a position, after your disgrace in Himyar?"

I could not believe Constantine was talking over my head, questioning my guide's loyalty, without knowing why I was here. I was used to standing aside and keeping my mouth shut. But I was the high king's daughter, and I was not used to being ignored.

"Constantine, hear me out," I said. "The kingship of Britain—"

My mistake was in stubbornly trying to make myself understood in Ethiopic. I had to work hard to follow it in conversation, and I could not speak it as well as I could understand it. In Latin I could have explained myself quickly. But Constantine cut off my stumbling story, all his attention now focused on Priamos.

"The prince Wazeb is Caleb's chosen heir, and my ward. I will not allow him to be threatened by the grasping of minor royalty," Constantine said. "If you so boldly defy the mandate of your uncle the emperor as his emissary in Britain, abandoning a post that many here think you did not deserve after you failed to defeat Abreha's army, what else can you be plotting?"

"I did not think I could be breaking my mandate in protecting the princess of Britain. But I see that I have," Priamos answered unhappily. "I never meant to do other than serve my uncle as he bid me. I was trained to it."

"Well, and so was the pretender Abreha, and that has not stood in the way of his treachery in Himyar!"

"I am not Abreha," said Priamos quietly.

"Yet after him you are the eldest son of Candake the queen of queens, the eldest of Caleb's nephews, and I find you here in violation of your commission."

"How am I Candake's eldest? What of Mikael?"

"Mikael!" Constantine laughed. "Mikael is insane."

"So should you be if you had spent the last thirty years shut up in the same three rooms!" Priamos burst out, in the most uncontrolled blaze of passion that I had ever seen from him.

There was a still, terrible moment while Constantine and Priamos faced each other, pale and dark, like a matched pair of opposing chessmen.

Then Constantine said in a flat voice, "You are under arrest for desertion. You will submit yourself to detainment in this house, or I will have you tried for apostasy against the empire's heir."

All this while I was struggling to understand the language. "Apostasy?" I asked desperately.

"Treason," whispered Priamos in Latin, stunned.

"I am regent here," Constantine went on. "I act for the king of kings Ella Asbeha, the emperor Caleb, as his viceroy

Ella Amida. You stand and challenge me in open defiance of my authority."

Constantine spoke, as he must have known, to the strict protocol of all Priamos's sequestered childhood and military training. Priamos, without seeming to show any kind of irony or insolence, knelt at Constantine's feet in the deep obeisance that he had made to my father when first they met, his hands open as if in supplication.

The boy in the white cotton cloak said suddenly, "You would be prone before your uncle the emperor."

"I submit to your authority," said Priamos, and lay flat on his chest, with his face sunken against his forearms.

Constantine gave a signal to his spear bearers. They moved to stand guard over Priamos, the bronze blades of their ceremonial spears held menacingly at his either side.

"Ras Priamos, you may have fought against Abreha under Caleb's orders, but you are still Abreha's brother," said Constantine. "Why he spared you and all your regiment is beyond my comprehension. He did not even try to ransom you. I cannot trust anyone so favored by the Himyarite pretender. My loyalty must lie with Wazeb."

"*Your loyalty lies with me,*" I interrupted in cold fury, hearing the frost in my voice as blowing straight down from the northern sea. "*How dare you.* How dare you stand cloaked in imperial robes not your own, in a palace not your own, with the royal spear bearers of a rival empire at your back, accusing your own sovereign's ambassador of treachery! You were to return to Britain next spring. Even if I had not meant to recall you, you would deliberately disobey Artos in seeing this command to its completion!"

Well, we were battling now, and openly, and not even in Latin, but in our common British dialect.

"Is that an accusation of treason, or your own interpretation of my actions?" Constantine said, barely controlling his fury. "On whose authority do you speak?"

"On my own," I said. "My God! That you should be wallowing in such splendor, while your sovereign lord and the sweet prince who was to fill your position here next year, my own twin, lay bleeding on the cold fields around Camlan! I traveled four thousand miles to reach you, who have been named my father's heir in the event of my brothers' deaths. Do you think anything less than the total destruction of my kingdom could have brought me here?"

Now Constantine seemed unsure how seriously to take me. "Do you mean to tell me—"

"Artos the high king of Britain is dead," I avowed, "and Lleu the young lion, the prince of Britain, slain in battle with him. Medraut, my father's eldest son, should have been our regent, as you know; but he, too, is lost. The king of the West Saxons is in control of our southern ports, the queen of the Orcades is grasping for what is left, and both have offered bounties for my capture. Britain's collapse is held in check by your own father and those of the high king's comrades who survived the battle of Camlan. . . ."

I took a breath and thumped my fists against my forehead in despair. "Oh, God, I have not the strength to repeat all of this in Ethiopic!"

I took another breath, trying to collect myself. Constantine and I stood face to face, but when I sought to hold his gaze he let his eyes slide away from mine, like all the people of this land.

"My father named you his heir in the event of his sons' deaths. Britain is yours for the taking," I said slowly, searching for appropriate words, "though I am now loath to bless your kingship with my hand in marriage, however long we have been promised."

The weight of my tale struck him now, and for a moment he shut his eyes, grimacing. Then he mastered himself and said evenly, "You are upset."

"I mean it," I swore, though by the terms of my father's legacy Constantine would be king whether or not I married him. He was the high king's eldest living nephew, and the high king's sons were dead.

"Would you spend your life in exile, battling against my reign, as Morgause did Artos?" Constantine asked, as though he were already crowned.

I answered coldly, "I do not need to seduce my brother to produce a queen's pawn, as she did when she created Medraut. I am Artos's own daughter. Any son I bear would have a greater claim than you to Britain's kingship."

"Don't covenant your unborn children," Constantine said contemptuously.

"Don't compare me to my aunt!"

We glared at each other.

Then Constantine gave a tired smile, and took my hands again, gently. "Forgive me, lady," he said, speaking Ethiopic himself, so that it would be understood by all and was something of a formal apology. "Your news has shocked and dazed me, and I am taking it in ill grace. I would not have greeted you so jestingly to begin with if I had known what news you bore."

"How can you know what news anyone bears before he tells it?" I said, and shook off his hands.

I glanced down at Priamos, who still lay flat on his face at our feet. I could see the gentle rise and fall of his back as he breathed; he lay quietly, not trembling or straining in any way, though the ceremonial spears biting into his ribs held him transfixed. Surely I had some authority over my own ambassador.

"Do you release Priamos Anbessa and make apology for the ill reception you have given him. He has most steadfastly served and protected me, and the prince of Britain as well."

Constantine spoke to his guards. "Withdraw your spears."

The spearmen ceased to threaten Priamos, and he got slowly to his feet. But the guards, who had not been dismissed, remained at his sides. Priamos did not raise his eyes; he showed no trace of defiance or injury.

"What was that all about?" the forward boy in white asked casually.

His regal self-assurance was so like my brother Lleu's that

I realized who he must be: this was Wazeb, Caleb's heir, whose kingdom Constantine was guarding. I noticed now that he was even crowned, after a fashion; his head cloth was bound with a simple circlet of twisted grass, whose points met in a cross.

"Artos the high king of Britain is dead," Constantine said in Ethiopic. He faced Priamos again. "For your safe delivery of the princess of Britain you have the gratitude of two kingdoms. But I must insist on your detainment here, until such time as you can prove to me surely that you are no threat to Wazeb's sovereignty."

Constantine turned to me. "And you, of course, my lady, we shall serve in any way we may, as best we can. We shall prepare you an apartment here—"

"Thank you, but I think not," I answered. "I have already accepted the hospitality of my brother's dear friends in the city. I think Kidane has less claim to royalty than Ras Priamos, and I trust you will not find my hosts guilty of any secret sedition."

"Come see me tomorrow morning. I am up to my neck in negotiations with the Beja tribesmen this afternoon. We can talk more privately in the morning, and decide what there is for us to do. You could meet me for the service at St. Mary of Zion, then break your fast with me. You'll like the cathedral."

"All right."

But our trust was in shards before it ever had a chance to set.

Other guards came in to escort Priamos out of the cham-

ber. He nodded a farewell to me, his expression impassive. If
he had tried to hold my gaze, I do not think I would have been
able to look at him; I felt as though I had led him into a trap.
But of course he did not try to meet my eyes. Our shared
tragedy at Camlan, our conspiratorial flight from Britain, our
partnered voyage, vanished like sea spray after a breaking
wave.

Telemakos was waiting in the corridor.

"Have you met your husband? What did you think of him?
Do you have to stay here longer, or will I bring you home to
meet my mother now?"

I could make no answer. I watched Priamos being led
away.

"Why is Ras Priamos under guard?"

I managed to collect myself, and answered with bitter
anger: "Because he is Abreha's brother, as you have pointed
out. Abreha was kind to him in Himyar, and Constantine
therefore thinks Priamos is not to be trusted."

"Kind to him!" Telemakos exclaimed. "Ras Priamos was
brought before Abreha naked and in chains after their battle.
So say his warriors."

"Yes, well, there is kindness and kindness. When your
enemy sends you home alive and free it counts as kindness."

"What did the viceroy say when you told him he was to be
high king of Britain?"

"Told me not to conceive my own nephew, like Morgause
the queen of the Orcades," I answered impulsively and inap-
propriately. Medraut was after all the child's father, beloved

though never known, a legend; like Odysseus to Telemakos's namesake.

The dark subtlety of my sarcasm was lost on Telemakos. He laughed, showing off his missing teeth. "Why would you need another nephew?" he asked. "You have me."

I stared at him. He was the high king's grandson, the only child of my father's eldest son.

"Why, so I have," I whispered.

CHAPTER III

✦

Coffee and Frankincense

THERE WAS A lion skin hanging in the reception hall of Kidane's mansion. Telemakos stopped below the skin and said, "This is my father's lion."

The skin covered nearly an entire wall. Its sightless eyes stared upward at the ceiling over snarling, bared teeth; the mane was black. All the pelt was dark, but it had an edge of gold that made it seem always changing color when you moved past.

"Ras Meder killed this himself, with a spear, and no one to guard or help him," Telemakos told me.

After a moment he added, "Gedar's children across the street don't believe that."

"Gedar's children never met your father," I said. "But I believe it."

Telemakos asked suddenly, "Did my father look like you?"

"We are alike, but not in looks," I answered. "Most of my family looked like me, dark-haired, dark-eyed; but Medraut—

what do you call him? Meder, Ras Meder, was more like you. His skin was fair as mine, but his hair and eyes were like yours."

"He's dead now," Telemakos stated frankly.

I hesitated. "He was wounded in the battle of Camlan," I said. "He was wounded in body and spirit, and we lost him after we buried our father."

Telemakos sank both hands deep in the dark fur of the lion skin, and stood silent. At last he pushed himself away from the wall and said evenly, "Look, here is my mother."

Turunesh was older than Priamos and I, younger than Medraut. She stood tall and calm. Her hair was fixed in many tiny plaits that lay close against her scalp, following the curve of her head, then billowing loose at her neck in an ebony cloud. Telemakos went to stand close to her side, beneath her arm, and she held him against her.

"This is my mother, Turunesh Kidane," said Telemakos.

She looked me up and down, taking in my travel-stained clothes and salt-spattered boots. "Peace to you, Princess Goewin," she said, in accented Latin. "Peace to you, little sister. You've been lost."

She held out her hand, and I took it. She touched my cheek to hers. I sighed.

"I am a disagreeable guest," I said. "I bring only evil news, and I have just had a roaring quarrel with my fiancé before half the imperial court."

"So did your brother, six years ago, when Constantine

arrived." Turunesh laughed, then stopped suddenly. She lifted
her hand from her son's shoulder to smooth down his thick,
luminous hair. "Have you brought me news of Medraut?"

"I cannot tell—"

Again I hesitated. I hated what I would have to tell her.
Throughout the last day I spent with Medraut he had not spoken a single word aloud.

Turunesh said gently, "It does not come as such a shock. I
thought it must be so, or you would not have traveled alone.
Tell me later, perhaps."

I sighed again. "I mean, I truly cannot tell," I said. "I do
not know what happened to him. I think Medraut took his
own life. I don't know. He's gone."

I dropped Turunesh's hand and knelt by her side, so that I
was level with Telemakos. He turned his head toward me. He
kept his eyes politely lowered, his expression quiet and still. I,
too, touched his bright hair.

"I would never have seen him anyway," Telemakos said.

"Ask Ferem to bring our supper in the garden," his mother told him. "And then coffee. You may eat with us, child, if
you do not talk, but straight to bed when the coffee is brought
out. You've been playing with the emperor's monkeys again,
haven't you? Go take a bath."

Telemakos bowed his head, then turned quickly and ran
past us into the house. I watched him go, my nephew.

We shared a meal without speaking. Darkness fell suddenly, and the butler Ferem lit lanterns that stood in standards

about the garden. The night seemed full of little noises: the soft, wet *pip-pip* of the ornamental fish breathing at the surface of the granite pool at my back, the slight ripple of the water as they dived again; moths and lizards fluttering and jumping in the thatched awning above our heads, the rustle of wind in the leaves of the giant sycamores. I dreaded my morning meeting with Constantine.

Ferem cleared away the baskets that had held the flat injera bread, and set before Turunesh a tray heavy with strange equipment: a small burner, a round and tall-necked earthen jug, a mortar, pans, and tiny earthen cups. The butler put a hand on Telemakos's shoulder, and the child stood up and let himself be led away to bed without protest.

I opened my mouth to ask, "What happens now?" and what came out was, "What happened in Himyar?"

"We were at war with them for seventeen years," Turunesh answered. "Himyar has alternated as our enemy and our ally longer than Aksum has been Christian, three hundred years or more. When their king began persecuting the Aksumite Christians there, Caleb defeated him and made the region a protectorate under a native viceroy. But the Aksumite settlers did not like Caleb's choice, so they threw the viceroy out and elected one of their own to take his place."

"Abreha."

"Yes."

"Why was Abreha in Himyar?"

"Caleb had sent him as a translator."

Have no trust in translators, I thought.

I asked aloud, "So then Caleb sent Priamos with an army to bring down Abreha?"

"Not at first. He sent his own son, Aryat, and Aryat was slain by Abreha. Then he sent Priamos's elder brother, Hector. Hector's force rebelled against him; he was very young. He was murdered by his own officers. Priamos's army fought after Hector's, and Abreha defeated him."

It was strange to sit in the dark courtyard, both of us tight with grief, and calmly discuss a war that had ended three years ago.

"They struck a truce," Turunesh finished. "Priamos was spared so that he might carry Abreha's message back to the emperor Caleb."

"Cynric used him in that exact way after Camlan," I said. "He was the only one of my father's men who knew anything of the Saxon tongue."

"That will not help his reputation at all," Turunesh commented, lighting the burner. "'Have no trust in translators,' Caleb used to say."

She blew gently on the flames in the brazier.

"Now watch," Turunesh said, straightening. "Let's no longer speak of Himyar. I am going to make you coffee. We'll drink in memory of your brother. He once told me he would give away a kingdom if it meant he might share another cup of coffee with me."

I saw her smiling over the blue and yellow flames.

"What is it?"

"A mild stimulant. It grows wild on the highland hillsides;

we roast and grind the seeds, then steep them to make a drink. Your brother hated it. But he liked the ceremony. Only a woman may make coffee. Watch."

She was busy as she spoke, deftly sorting the seeds. They rattled musically against the earthen pan she held them in; the flames of the burner whiffled and leapt. I could not ever remember being so aware of the light, quiet sounds of a garden at night.

Perhaps because I was listening so intently, perhaps because the cool highland air and rustling sycamores and bitter scent of roasting coffee were so strange to me, I heard a thing Turunesh did not hear. Behind me, below the gentle breathing of the fish, I heard the gentle breathing of another small creature. Turunesh began to pulverize the seeds in the mortar. I lowered my head, slowly, and glanced sideways back over my arm.

There was a border of tall flowers along one edge of the pool; their leaves were nearly black in the darkness, and all was black beneath their leaves. I sat with my head bent, as though lost in thought, and let my eyes adjust to the dark.

Turunesh lifted the roasting pan from the burner and set the water in the fat pot to boil. The flames soared, crackling around the bottom of the jug. Their sudden flaring lit a shape beneath the leaves with a faint edge of silver, and for one second I could see that Telemakos lay there as stone himself, his chin resting on his hands and his eyes closed. I only saw him for a second. He seemed at ease lying in the soil beneath the tall flowers, and he might have been asleep; but something in the alert angle of his still head told me that he was wide awake, and listening, listening.

For a few moments I did not move my head either, so that I should not let him know I had discovered him. I had seen Telemakos take enough mild blows and rebukes in one day that I had no heart to call him out. He could listen if he liked.

"What is that smell?" I murmured.

"The coffee?"

"More like perfume. Familiar . . . "

"Frankincense, perhaps? There is a plantation on the hillside above this suburb. Our priests burn it as incense; your own may do the same."

"Yes, so they do. I recognize it now."

I sat sorting out the strange smells and sounds. The light, even breathing went on steadily behind me, scarcely perceptible. But I did not notice when it stopped. Telemakos was not there when we went to bed: I never heard him coming or going. He moved with the sure and absolute silence of a leopard stalking its prey.

In the cathedral the next morning the frankincense was overpowering. Clouds of it rose from the censers swung by the priests in their red-bordered robes; the gilt wings of the angels painted on the ceiling seemed to float in haze. Constantine stood at my side as we listened to the morning service.

The chanting, the drumbeat and rattle of sistrums, was strange to my ears. I stood looking up at the mild, wide-eyed, host that flew across the vaulted ceiling on gold wings. As the service ended and the assembly began to process out, Constantine whispered in Latin, close to my ear, "Marry me now."

I had to bite the knuckle of my index finger, hard, to keep from bursting into laughter. It did not seem to merit an answer, there and then.

"Marry me here, in this church, before the rains end."

No. I shaped the word soundlessly with my lips.

Constantine tilted his head, pretentious in his Aksumite beard and head cloth. "What did you say?" he whispered.

"No!" I said aloud. All the people around gave me oblique glances and quickly looked away again. I took a deep breath of the cloying incense. We followed the priests out into the misty highland morning.

In the time it took us to cross the cathedral square, Constantine and I had collected a following of what seemed like dozens of beggars: an eyeless, limbless group of mutilated men, some young, some older. They called to me in Greek and Ethiopic.

"Sister! Sister! Foreign lady, sister!"

They reached beseeching hands but did not try to touch me, not daring to come into range of the ceremonial spear bearers.

I turned frowning to Constantine and asked, "Why are the beggars all so badly maimed?"

"They are veterans of the Himyar," he answered briefly. "I

have tried to find employment and hospice for them, but there are too many. Ras Priamos's legacy to Aksum."

"The emperor Caleb's legacy, surely," I corrected.

"Of course, you're right. Himyar embitters me. Caleb depleted his nation's treasury and youth in conflict there, and I am left to sweep up the debris."

I wondered what he had done. He had not held this office for more than a half year, after all. Anything he did for Aksum he might also do for Britain.

"Tell me," I said, testing him.

"I've converted the old palace to an asylum for returning soldiers. I donated a boatload of my father's tin to pay for it."

"That is very generous of your father," I said.

He did not answer that. We walked the rest of the way to the New Palace without a word.

We broke our fast together in a small room that was bright with bowls of flowers. I thought of Constantine's proposal, and it made me want to laugh again. I bit my lip, embarrassed. He was trying to be courteous.

"What have you done for Aksum that you are proudest of?" I asked, trying hard myself.

"I have stopped the Beja tribes skirmishing over where their emeralds are sold, and curbed the banditry along the Salt Road," he answered. "But I am most proud of this."

He undid a purse by his side and passed to me a small and shining coin. It was curiously beautiful, copper daubed with gold, a broad cross imprinted with a sunburst at its heart.

"That is the new issue in bronze. I used my own tin in the minting of them. I have not enjoyed my tenure here," Constantine confessed. "But I serve as I am able. I think I have done some little good as Ella Amida."

"Why do you call yourself Ella Amida?"

"It was the title of the reigning negus when Constantine the Great was emperor of Rome, two hundred years ago, when Rome and Aksum became Christian."

Constantine leaned across the table toward me. "Goewin, I meant what I said this morning. I think we should get married now. It would simplify a great deal, and it would set me free of the Aksumite regency."

"I am not handing over my father's kingdom so easily," I answered.

Constantine paused. Then he took my hand and held it clasped lightly between us on the table, as he continued his gentle, obstinate persuasion. "Goewin, I shall not force you. And I don't want to coerce you. But you have nothing without me. You have no following, no army, no great income—"

"Telemakos," I interrupted.

"Excuse me?"

"I have Telemakos," I said. My voice sounded cold and calm in my own ears.

For several long moments he did not speak.

"What can you mean?" he said at last.

With my hand still clasped beneath Constantine's, I let these words spill steady and quiet from some dark place in my heart:

"I have Telemakos. My father would not let the kingship pass to Medraut, not because he was illegitimate, but because he was the child of incest. Telemakos is removed from that. He is the son of the high king's eldest son. Who would deny that he has a greater claim to the British throne than you, or even I?"

Constantine said in astonishment, "Telemakos is Aksumite!"

I leaned toward him so that we stared across the table into each other's eyes. I held his gaze. "You are British," I said, "and no one questions your place on the Aksumite throne. What makes you think anyone will question Telemakos in Britain? He is the high king's grandson. I am his daughter. Who are you?"

"Is that a challenge?"

"You may take it as one," I said.

Constantine stood up and paced to the window. There was a bowl of small white highland roses sitting on the sill. He stood there a long time, still, looking down at the roses.

He said at last, "Have you a plan that goes with your posturing threat?"

"You let me choose Britain's king myself, regardless of our marriage," I answered straightaway. "Or I take Telemakos to Britain as high king in waiting, and sever our alliance with Aksum's viceroy."

"You can't do that," Constantine snapped. "My wealth comes through my father, and I do not need the high king's benediction to gift Aksum with it."

"What you do as a private citizen is your own concern.

You will have no military support from your king, no treaty, no royal sanction, no ambassador."

"You fled Britain because Morgause wanted you dead. What will stop her from killing both you and your child minion?"

I answered through clenched teeth.

"He's her grandson."

Constantine suddenly picked up the roses and dropped the bowl out the window. I heard the crack of ceramic on the ground outside.

"Excuse me," Constantine said. "I have much to attend to this morning."

"I, too," I said. "I want to speak with my ambassador. Where can I find Priamos?"

"He is in council with the bala heg. They will be in session until dark, and again tomorrow. Come back in two days, if you want to see him." He paced to the door. "You will not mind if I leave you here to finish on your own."

CHAPTER IV

✦

Accounting

COME BACK IN *two days.* Tell me another, I thought in fury, sitting alone over the remains of the breakfast. I pushed back my chair and stood up. The young man who had been waiting on us came forward politely. "May I guide you somewhere?"

I thought hard, then said in precise and careful Ethiopic, "I need to find the emperor's linguist."

Halen, the afa negus or "mouth of the king," held the position that Priamos had been trained to fill. He had been Priamos's tutor once. I had to wait for him, of course, as I had to wait for everyone, but after an hour or so he came to meet me in the Golden Court.

"How can I help you, Princess?" Halen asked in polite Latin. "Have you need of an interpreter? I cannot leave this palace, but I can make you a recommendation."

"I want your recommendation," I answered, "but not in

the way you mean. Listen. You are not forbidden to talk to Priamos, are you? When will you see him next?"

"He did invite me to lunch with him in his room," Halen answered mildly.

"May I join you?"

"He was so evil-tempered a companion yestereve that I would not advise it," Halen said wryly, and I suddenly liked him.

"So am I, of late. No one will notice."

"Then meet me here again this noon, Princess."

Halen escorted me at midday to Priamos's chamber.

The room was small, but comfortably and even luxuriously furnished, high up and with a breathtaking view of the city and the distant Simien Mountains. Neither door nor window was barred, but there were guards posted outside. Halen and I stood waiting while one of these went in to announce us. As the soldier entered the room I saw that Priamos was deeply asleep, lying fully clothed, with his forearm flung across his eyes to block out the light.

"Wait—" I began, but too late, for the guard had already awakened him, and impassively moved to take up his station again.

Halen stood back, and Priamos greeted me alone.

"Peace to you, Princess," he said, and rose to his feet. "Come in."

I took his hands and answered, "You've been lost."

We stood and stood, both of us staring down at our clasped hands. The sun-browned skin of my own seemed fair and pale with Priamos's earth-dark fingers closed around them. His bony wrists were crossed with little scars that I had never noticed before, smooth and faintly shining, like the marks of burns or abrasions.

"Halen," I said, glancing back over my shoulder.

Priamos looked up. His tutor stood in the doorway. Priamos turned away from me and gestured to a chair.

"Come in, sir."

"I'll go now, Priamos," Halen said, speaking in Latin still. "Be good to the princess."

He turned away and left. The guards stood impassively, unblinking.

"Please, sit. Eat, if you like."

On the low table by the couch a tray of food had been set, still covered with a cotton cloth but no longer steaming. Beside it was a basket of fresh fruit. None of it had been touched.

"But it's yours," I said.

"I will not eat," Priamos said. "I only have an hour."

He had been *asleep*. What meeting could be so important or exhausting that he set aside food for an hour's sleep?

"What have they been doing with you?" I could not keep the anger from my voice.

"I have been standing in interview since dawn this morning, and from noon to dusk yesterday as well. It leaves me with no appetite."

"What interview?"

"Please do sit," he said dispiritedly, with a glance at the

open door where the guards waited. He was furnished with every comfort but had no privacy, and he did not want anyone to think he was being discourteous to his foreign and royal guest.

So I sat, while Priamos remained on his feet as though he were my butler.

"Constantine told me you are in council with the bala heg."

"Yes. We are discussing the resolution of my appointment in Britain."

"For two solid days?"

"I left so much undone," Priamos said, and moved to gaze out the high window. "I am not able to account for anything that was entrusted to me."

"You have accounted for *me*," I said, but stopped. I had seen with what gratitude Constantine had welcomed him. "What have you left undone?" I asked instead.

Priamos spoke as though reciting, still gazing out the window.

"There was a shipment of your tin from Dumnonia, that I was to deliver here. There was the shipment that was lost last year, for which I was to arrange repayment or replacement. There was your father's man who had resigned his post as envoy to Justinian, the Roman emperor, and Caleb bid me urge Artos to appoint someone to fill his place, as your Roman envoy is our nearest link to Britain. I had brought with me to Britain an ark filled with coins in silver and bronze, which

Artos wanted to circulate, a trove worth as much as another boatload of tin, and I have no idea what happened to it. . . ."

He stopped to draw breath.

"Nothing has happened to it," I said. "After Camlan it was moved into the copper mines for safekeeping, with all the other treasury. Do you remember Caius, my father's steward? He has charge of it."

Priamos turned to me. "Thank you, Princess," he said. "That will be a help this afternoon."

"Must they see you this afternoon yet? What more can there be?"

"It has surprised me how much there is. All little things I have forgotten, what has happened to the presents I brought with me for Artos, what could Artos suggest that Caleb give you as a wedding gift. Caleb's miserable lions, I am accountable for them. Horses, Artos was to send some of his horses here, and samples of their shoes, and the queen of queens had asked for more of that liqueur you make of those little sour plums . . ."

"Sloes."

"Yes. And this afternoon I am to report to Ella Amida the present state of Britain."

"Ella Amida. You mean Constantine . . ." I spoke slowly. "Has he been questioning you all this time?"

"Oh, indeed not. He steps in and out. He is very busy. He has set aside much to spare this afternoon for me. . . ." Priamos drew another long breath. "Nothing has been raised that I could not have foreseen if I had thought about it—"

(If he had thought about anything during our voyage other than satisfying my demands to learn Ethiopic, or ensuring I was not ambushed by Saxon spies.)

"Yet I fear it will not end till Constantine has seen me stripped and flogged in the Cathedral Square."

"I do not understand why he should so distrust you."

"Because I am so like Abreha. We were both trained as translators, favored by Caleb. And because Abreha himself killed Caleb's eldest son, Aryat. Do you see? Everyone fears that Abreha's brother will betray Aryat's brother in the same way, that I will bring harm to Wazeb. Constantine is not alone in his distrust. It is not the first time I have been taxed with my failure in Himyar."

Priamos sighed. "Yet so much of this present trial seems so trivial. I have offered my own lands and estate in payment for the lost imports. But I cannot believe that my life and career are to end in ignominy because I—" He choked, breathless. "Because I failed to send half a dozen jars of wine to my gluttonous mother!"

We both laughed wildly.

"Do sit down," I said, biting my lip at my own lunatic behavior.

Priamos sat on the floor at my feet, finally, with his long legs drawn up against his chest and his arms clasped around his knees. He sighed again, and we sat still and silent for a few moments, apart, but drawing strength and solace from our shared laughter.

"My mother wants to meet you," Priamos said at last. "I

took coffee with her last night. I think you will like Candake the queen of queens, if she does not scare you to death first. You might visit with her this afternoon, while I am in tribunal."

"I will not. I shall be there with you."

He began to protest, sober now.

"I will not be ruled by you, or anyone," I said. "I have more sway over Constantine than he cares to admit, and I will not hear of the state of Britain being discussed behind my back."

"What have you over Constantine?"

I hesitated, then answered softly, "One who might be called prince of Britain."

It felt strange to speak these words and mean what I meant by them.

Priamos shook his head without understanding. "The prince of Britain died at Camlan."

"I don't mean Lleu," I said. "I mean Telemakos Meder. He is the high king's grandson."

"Oh."

Priamos shook his head again.

He said slowly, "The boy has his own title; did you know? He is formally Lij Telemakos, which is something equivalent to young prince, a child of noble birth. He is heir to the house of Nebir. No one ever uses his title, though."

Then he added, "You are playing a dangerous game."

"I know it," I said. "But I have no other strength. Oh! Would I were a man!"

Priamos rubbed one hand savagely down his face from temple to jaw and across his mouth, as though he were trying to wipe his face off. "Would I were a different man," he said passionately.

It is not easy getting yourself into the innermost council chamber of the New Palace uninvited, but certain outrageous or persuasive people have succeeded in it once or twice. I managed at last, making the most of my title and my position as Kidane's guest and Constantine's promised bride. They were well under way when I came in, and there was a flurry of confusion while they set an extra chair for me at the side of Constantine's throne. Constantine glared at me murderously throughout this disturbance. The crown prince Wazeb was there as well, sitting straight and silent, as though it were a great show performed for his entertainment.

The questions of the bala heg were fair. A few of the council must have had some sympathy for Priamos; I am sure that his brother Ityopis did, and Kidane. But it was an interrogation that fell just short of torture, and even so I think they dealt with Priamos more kindly while I was there. He stood for hours, with the patience of a lifetime's training, before the knot of seated nobles. Not one of them remained in the room for the length of the session; they came and went as they grew weary, or had other appointments to keep. They had drink and sweets brought to them as they listened. Priamos alone remained on his feet without respite, like a prisoner.

My presence must have made the court even more tedious: for now everything had to be asked twice, first by a councilor in Ethiopic, and then again in Latin, for my benefit, by Halen. In an exquisite additional humiliation, Priamos was expected to translate his own answers. I hated that my very ignorance made this trial more difficult for Priamos, so that in everything he said he should be doubly checked by Constantine and by the translator, the afa negus. But I could not have followed it without Halen's assistance, particularly when they spoke of numbers: how many men were left in Cynric's force after the battle of Camlan, what the number of cattle and the weight in gold that Cynric had offered for my bride price. I sat absorbed in concentration, working at understanding the questions on my own, leaning forward as though it would make their words clearer if I were closer to the speakers.

Priamos had surrendered himself voluntarily to Cynric, a thing which was found to be deeply improbable, and not just by Constantine.

"I should think," said Danael, the one of the bala heg who seemed to be the assembly's leader, "that after being sent home in disgraced bondage from the Himyar, you would not be anxious to become captive again; and yet you submit yourself, untaken, to the warlord who came against the king you were sent to serve."

Ityopis, who stayed in session longer than any of the rest, put in, "He was not sent from Himyar in disgrace. He was sent free, with Ahreha's pardon."

"He was sent free by Cynric, as well, and I will know why there was so much goodwill all around, in the wake of a battle that resulted in the death of Britain's high king."

So Priamos explained how it had started by mistake, and how a settlement had been reached before it began, and how he had hoped to discover the prince of Britain's fate through his own surrender. He took full responsibility for his actions, and I thought he acquitted himself well.

When Constantine spoke, he always seemed to ask things that Priamos could not possibly know, or which Constantine should know himself.

"You have said the southern ports are in Cynric's hands: which are the southern ports?"

"Has Cynric allegiances among the Saxon pirates?"

"What was the strength of the Deva garrison before it was reduced?"

What did that matter?

"What is the present strength of the Deva garrison?" asked Danael.

Priamos waited patiently for the question to be translated for me before making an answer.

"I cannot guess with any accuracy," he said in Ethiopic.

There was a long silence.

"I cannot guess with any accuracy," Priamos repeated in Latin.

"You cannot guess?"

"I do not know." There was another long pause. Priamos sighed, and translated. "I do not know."

"Guess without accuracy," suggested Constantine.

Priamos said hesitantly, "Two thousand, perhaps."

"Closer to twenty-five hundred," I said in Latin, "with five hundred more relocated to Melandra."

There was a moment of frozen quiet.

Before anyone could repeat or translate my answer, Constantine asked, "How do you know that?"

"I ordered it," I said, and straightened my back. I had been leaning forward for so long, with such intense concentration, that my neck ached. "I ordered the dispersal of all the infantry that fought at Camlan. As I ordered Caleb's trove of silver to be locked in the underground vaults at Elder Field, near Camlan." I turned to the afa negus. "Do you tell them what I said."

If I had not been so outraged at their criminal treatment of Priamos, I would have laughed at the court's reaction when Halen repeated my speech. Wazeb did laugh, out loud and in delight. He had straight teeth that were bright in his dark face, and a smile that came and went as quickly as lightning in a thunderhead.

Zoskales, the eldest of the council, asked in Ethiopic, "Who is she?"

The translator did not repeat this. I realized that half of them assumed I did not understand a word that was spoken unless it was in my own language.

I answered the question in Ethiopic. "I am Goewin the dragon's daughter. I am the only living child of the king whose wealth you have discussed all this afternoon."

Priamos, who had not yet spoken a word unless it was required of him, said now: "She is rightfully high queen of Britain, negeshta nagast, queen of kings. It shames me that we are not all on our knees before her." He added recklessly, "And he who calls himself Ella Amida will not come into his own inheritance without her blessing."

It threw them into uproar. Most of them came to their feet; Kidane and another three bowed, including Danael and Ityopis. Two more began to rise, then sat again.

"Who let her in, then?" the old man muttered. "I do not understand who let her in."

"SHE IS DAUGHTER TO THE KING OF BRITAIN," his neighbor bellowed at his ear.

"She is the viceroy's betrothed. She is the viceroy's betrothed," said Priamos in Ethiopic and in Latin. In the frantic astonishment that followed, Priamos enthusiastically repeated this last in Greek and Arabic, and finally, for good measure, in Hebrew.

Wazeb gave another bark of delight.

"*We will come to order!*" Constantine thundered. "Zoskales, do you sit on this council to prescribe laws or to nap? And you, Ras Priamos, I swear, if I am made to endure one more insolence from you I will set you to cutting salt blocks in the desert for the next two years, *do not doubt me.* Now let us finish this! I cannot spare another afternoon—"

"You have a season of afternoons to spare," I blazed, and I was on my feet with the rest of them. It was all I could do to keep from striking him in the teeth. "The long rains are upon us. I may have no jurisdiction over Priamos in this land, but by my father's sword, I am your queen, Constantine. Ella Amida. Whoever you are. Detain Priamos here if you must, but save for me your questions over my father's wealth and the size of his armies! We shall discuss Britain at length before either of us is able to travel there. You may schedule interviews with me over all this season, but I will see an end to this inquisition of my ambassador!" I sat down and added, "Now, shall you exile me for insolence?"

It was the end. There were no more questions. Priamos was taken back to his room, and Kidane and I walked home together through pouring rain.

PART II

STALEMATE

CHAPTER V

✦

A Red Sea Itinerary

"WHY ARE YOU sad?" Telemakos said to me suddenly.

I stood in Kidane's reception hall, arms folded, staring out the tall windows at the dripping forecourt. Telemakos was trying to teach one of the parrots to whistle as he did, through the gap in his teeth.

"You look sad," he repeated.

"The rain makes me homesick," I told him. "What do you do all winter?"

"Beg Grandfather to take me to the New Palace with him," Telemakos answered readily, in between whistles.

"What is there to entertain you in the New Palace?"

"I play gebeta and santaraj with the queen of queens. And I play with the animals. Candake has very clever cats: we make them do tricks. She tells good stories, too. I like the queen of queens. She is beautiful." He whistled again, speaking absently, concentrated on the parrot. He had an unintentional habit of narrowing his eyes and lifting one white eyebrow when he was focused on something, which made him seem deceptively calculating and precocious.

"I help the animals keeper," Telemakos continued. "And—" He whistled, and laughed, because this time the parrot answered him. "Well done, Rainbow!"

"And?" I prompted.

"I like to listen to the courtiers."

"Don't they mind?"

"They never notice," he said casually. "Grandfather is always telling me to listen."

"Do you hide sometimes?"

Still coaxing the parrot, Telemakos did not blink or falter; but he did not answer me immediately.

"I might," he said at last, "sometimes. If Grandfather were looking for me, perhaps." He laughed again. "I'm always hiding from Grandfather.

"You should come with me when I visit the queen of queens," he added. "She will want to play with your hair, and she always has the best sweets."

"I will," I said decisively. "I have to go tomorrow to talk to Constantine, anyway. And I want to see Priamos again."

The guards at Priamos's door bowed politely to me and ushered us through. We found him sitting on the floor of his room, sorting through a heap of books in at least five languages.

"Ah, Princess, how kind of you to bring me entertainment!" Priamos exclaimed. "I have read all of these a dozen times apiece."

"Why don't you walk about the palace more?"

"I cannot go anywhere without the imperial guard breathing down my neck. I would as soon stay here. My childhood at Debra Damo has accustomed me to stricture."

I could not understand the stricture of his childhood. I asked, "Why were you sent there, Priamos?"

"It is traditional," he said mildly. "The emperor's male relatives are always closely guarded, so we may not overthrow him. My brother Mikael, eldest son of the queen of queens, will never be set free. A good many think Caleb a madman to have been so generous toward the rest of his sister's sons."

"They say the same of my mother," Telemakos agreed with sympathy, pushing aside the books so he might sit cross-legged on the floor next to Priamos. "The queen of queens is always telling me how lucky I am not to be sequestered myself. She says it happens, sometimes, to noble children whose fathers disappear."

What a strange world you live in, I thought.

Telemakos began picking up books also, opening them and making little grunts of distaste or dismissal as he discovered the contents of each.

"If I were imprisoned in this palace, I would stay always in the Golden Court," I said. "It's so light there, and I love the sound of the fountains."

"Pah!" Priamos made a gesture of disgust. "I hate the

Golden Court. All those chained monkeys. They make me sick."

"I like the monkeys," Telemakos said.

"It is the chains I object to."

Priamos glared down at his disordered books. I knelt to stack them for him.

"How long will your detention last?" I asked. "We were going to hunt together."

"We may yet. We could not go now in any case, while the rains persist."

"Rain makes the princess homesick," Telemakos said. "Is it really like this in Britain, all the year long? I should hate it. I like to be outside."

"So do your monkeys."

We both gazed down at Telemakos's shining head, bent in concentration over Priamos's books. It was as though I held this child tethered by an invisible lead, a chain even lighter and stronger than the gold that bound the monkeys. He did not know he wore it, but I held him captive and condemned as if the links were real.

Telemakos seemed to pay no notice to either of us. Priamos rubbed one of his narrow hands around the opposite wrist and looked up.

"How have you entertained yourself since your arrival in Aksum, Princess?" he asked me.

"Constantine and I meet every day. We've got half a dozen meetings scheduled over the next week; we are supposed to work out a plan for my return to Britain."

Sifting through documents in his office, Constantine and I tried to piece together what we still owed Aksum in borrowed revenue or goods not paid for. Behind Constantine's records in his files were other documents, written in Ethiopic or Greek, but signed or annotated in Latin in Medraut's firm, spare hand. Medraut had rarely put his name to anything, I came to realize; he signed himself anonymously "Ambassador of Britain" or "Envoy of Artos." His record keeping was complicated and meticulous, but Constantine had made a faithful attempt to equal it. I would never grow to like Constantine, yet I was beginning to see why Caleb thought he would make a decent viceroy, and even why my father had placed him in line for the British kingship.

Wazeb was always there as well, listening without watching us, his head tilted to one side as Halen whispered brief translations at his ear. Once, when Constantine and I had become embroiled in yet another bitter argument, Constantine had turned to Wazeb and said apologetically, "We dishonor you, debating so in your company."

"Not at all," Wazeb had answered lightly. "It is very interesting."

It made my neck go tense, thinking about it.

"Constantine has wealth my father did not have," I said to Priamos. "I have allegiances his father does not have. And I know where my father's soldiers are stationed, and their numbers and strengths, and which parts of Mercia had an abundant harvest last year and so on—but I dislike Constantine so much I don't want to tell him anything. We scarcely greet each other before we are battling, and we get nowhere, and each day we begin again at the beginning. I have said I will not marry him unless he lets me choose an heir."

"Ah, queen of kings indeed!" Priamos laughed. "A princess at liberty to choose her father's heir! How you have turned your weakness to your advantage. Or is it more like a hostage negotiation?"

"That," I said, and reached to take the book Telemakos held, "that is a thing we do not talk about." I closed the book and put it aside. Telemakos picked it up again. "I grow weary of my fruitless interviews with Constantine. We will have nothing to say to each other long before winter is over."

"You must think of some occupation," said Priamos. "I am teaching the tame lion to read the testaments in Greek."

"Teaching the tame lion to read Greek? What are you talking about?"

"It is my mother's name for Wazeb," Priamos said. "It is a greater compliment than you might think. A tame lion is less predictable than a chained one. Isn't that right, young lion tamer?"

Telemakos did not answer. He was frowning studiously over the volume I had tried to take from him. He cried, "Oh, look at this!" and began to unfold a page. Spread out, it entirely covered his lap. "Oh, what is this a map of? I can't read Greek either—"

I bent over his shoulder. It was a map of the world.

"Here's Aksum—" I pointed "—where we are now. And

here is Britain, where I come from. I can show you the way we traveled, look, starting up here, following the coast past Britanny and Iberia—"

We were both suddenly absorbed. Telemakos held the map open, his touch light and careful. He watched my finger tracing its path across the papyrus and nodded as I listed the Mediterranean ports where we had stopped.

Priamos watched us. When I looked up at him again he said, "I did not know *you* read Greek."

"I don't. My mother was a mapmaker. She taught me to draw the projections in Ptolemy's *Geography*. I can't read the names, but I know the map very well. What is this book?"

"It's a *Red Sea Itinerary*. It's a shipping guide. I wish we'd had this on our voyage; it might have stopped you always questioning our route."

"I only questioned when you suddenly changed our route, before I knew we were followed. Look, Telemakos, here is Gabaza, the customs point for ships arriving at Adulis. I thought I would not be able to breathe, it was so hot when we landed there. It was so strange to me. But there was another white passenger on our ship, a merchant sailor who could not speak, and while I was waiting to disembark I watched him making his way through the crowd on the quay. He gave me courage. I'd never met him face-to-face; I only ever saw his back. But he gave me courage. He walked haltingly, like the rest of us, unused to land beneath his legs, but he moved with such confidence and purpose. I thought that if a man who could not speak was able to face strangers so fearlessly, then so should I be able to. And see, when I arrived, there were no strangers after all. There was you."

"Show me how you came here from Adulis," Telemakos demanded.

"Goodness, haven't you had enough of maps yet?"

"I love maps," Telemakos answered promptly.

Priamos laughed. "Well, see, both of you. I bought this edition because of the maps."

He lifted the book from Telemakos's lap and folded the wide sheet back in place. "Here is the road from Adulis to Aksum," Priamos said, turning pages over. "And look, let me show you my favorite. Here is the road to Debra Damo, the cliff top hermitage where I and my brothers were sequestered."

The picture was so stylized that you could scarcely call it a map: it showed an entire landscape. The road was drawn as a thin line with a cross marked at either end, and hatchings and bends here and there to mark turnings along the way. Around the road were miniature sketches of trees and animals and villages, all leading to a wide plateau with a geometric Aksumite church perched on its flat height. Below the church there lurked a serpent the size of an elephant, stretching its fearsome coils up the cliff side.

"What on earth is that?" I asked. "Have they got a dragon to guard you there?"

"The saint who founded the monastery was lifted to the top of the amba plateau by a flying serpent," Priamos said. "Or so the stories say. In its place now they have a leather rope. There is no other way in or out."

"You'd be very safe," said Telemakos.

"Some people go there for sanctuary," Priamos said. "But my brother Mikael has spent his life imprisoned there, and that is not the same thing at all."

Priamos closed the book and reached out to lay it atop one of the stacks I had made. Beneath his shamma his arms were bare, and I noticed again the small, slick scars on his wrists. They were so faded you could only see them when they caught the light.

"Goewin wants to meet your mother," Telemakos said. "Will you take us to her, Ras Priamos?"

"That I will do with pleasure, Telemakos Meder. I may not stay, though."

Candake the queen of queens, negeshta nagashtat, was enormous. I have since heard many people call her beautiful, as Telemakos did, and so she is; but still Caleb's elder sister was bigger than any human being I have ever seen. She must have weighed as much as a small buffalo. She was not able to move as quickly as a buffalo, though, and was surrounded by a swarm of attendants who helped her to sit and to stand, and who seemed to feed her constantly. Her hair had gone salt white, and there were dozens of fine gold chains woven into her tight plaits. She was wonderful, and terrifying; in her own way, eerily, much like my aunt Morgause.

"Ah, you bring her to me at last, Priamos! How I have longed to see this girl! The queen of queens beholds the—what did you call her in the tribunal?"

"Queen of kings," Telemakos supplied.

I wondered, Where did you pick up that?

"The queen of kings." Candake creased and cackled with uncontrollable laughter, and leaned forward to grab Telemakos's hands and swing them back and forth as though she were dancing with him. "Queen of kings! Like Cleopatra!" I thought she was going to choke herself laughing. "Or Makeda, the queen of Sheba, the mother of us all! Ah, Priamos, no other of my children could have been destined to speak as the mouth of the king; you have the flyaway tongue of a catbird.

"Girl, do you know what he said when he came before my brother Caleb for the first time, what he called the negus? 'Solomon,' he said. 'Solomon walks among us in your wisdom.' And Caleb said it was bad enough he had a base traitor in one nephew, without another being a groveling sycophant."

"My lady mother, I am supposed to go and repeat to my old tutor what little I have learned of the British tongue," Priamos interrupted quickly. "I will leave you alone with the princess."

Candake paused for breath, chuckling and wheezing. "Priamos was sick, sick with nerves. After the presentation to Caleb they took the children out to see the animals, and he vomited into the lion pit."

One of Priamos's guards was twitching in his attempt to keep a straight face. "Go, go!" Priamos said to them, turning quickly. "Tedla, Ebana, I swear I'll have you whipped for insolence. Go! I am late." He drove the guards before him with his arms spread wide, abandoning me to his mother.

"Coward!" I called after him, laughing.

"No coward," his mother grunted darkly. "He will find little time for idle sport this winter. The bala heg are going to keep him busy."

Telemakos settled himself comfortably at the grand woman's feet. He leaned low to the floor and chirruped softly. Three slender cats the color of sand, with faint stripes across their noses and tails, came slinking out from beneath baskets and behind curtains and swarmed over his lap. One of them perched on his shoulder, rubbing its head against his face and purring so violently you could have heard it from across the room.

"You may trust my handmaids, little Sheba," Candake told me kindly. "Say what you like; who shall repeat it outside this court shall have her tongue cut out."

She patted Telemakos on top of his head with one of her fat, painted hands. "Isn't that right, my fox kit?"

He tossed his head. "You don't scare me," he said loftily. "And anyway—I'm no telltale."

They had to say everything two or three times over before I could fully understand it, but I think that is how it went. Candake made me sit at her feet opposite Telemakos. Then, tilting my chin toward her with one thick, emerald-laden finger, the queen of queens demanded: "Tell me, Princess of Britain, have you met my sweet nephew, the good and holy Wazeb, heir to the king of kings? A king-priest shall we have in him, not a bad thing, though his father thinks him a very silly boy. And what think you of our salt-faced regent? Let me touch your hands while we speak, your smooth pale hands. Constantine will not let me near him."

I thought she had some important things to tell me, implied in her pregnant questions. I let her stroke my hands, fascinated by her.

"Can you explain—" I ventured. "Can you tell me how Constantine came to power here?"

"Through my brother having the temperament of a hyena." Candake snickered. One of the maids began to feed her pieces of fruit cut into stars and crescents and diamonds. "Why should Caleb work when another can do it for him? Hyena! Caleb sent one after another of my sons into battle, so to avoid losing any more of his own. The day my husband Anbessa died, even before he was lying in his grave, Caleb sent the order that my sons should be released from their sequestering and brought to him to train as his warriors. My brother has emptied his treasury on war and this palace. He looks at his heir and sees that Wazeb chants and dreams of God. Caleb mourns his lost Aryat, and thinks his ravaged kingdom will fall to a son without ambition or ability.

"So Caleb designs to retire to the dragon's hermitage and let another patch up his empire for him, while Wazeb waits his chance at power. But Wazeb will not grasp and grab at authority. Ha! You watch him. The tame lion. And they think all the lions have gone from the emperor's palace!" She gave another burst of elephantine laughter.

"So Caleb looks about him for a regent, saying, Which of these attendant insects will suck up the most nourishment for Aksum, before he begins to whine so irritatingly that Wazeb is forced to snatch up the imperial fly whisk? Caleb reviews them all and fixes on the mosquito Constantine. No one else is so strict, so plodding and pedantic. And no one is so dispensable. So they go up to Mai Shum with the bishop, the abuna, and a cloud of priests, and in the reservoir they baptize Constantine again with our own baptism, and so you see him now, the viceroy Ella Amida."

Candake stopped speaking at last, wheezing.

"So if Constantine fails, the blame is Constantine's," I said. "And if he succeeds, the kingdom is Wazeb's. Whatever happens, no reproof will come to Caleb. It is not so unaccountable as it looks."

"A princess and a politician!" Candake chuckled. "Bring coffee. Feed some of those to the princess," she ordered suddenly; and to my consternation, the maid began to put the fruit stars into my mouth.

"How long will Wazeb endure it?" I asked, when I could. "Does he seem likely to snatch up the fly stick?"

"Fly stick!" Candake creased herself laughing again. "Why should he put down his prayer stick? It is good enough for swatting flies, and his British viceroy is bringing order and wealth to the mess his father left behind him. The tame lion will wait and watch."

Then she screamed for the coffee to be brought.

"Where's that boy gone?" Candake demanded suddenly. "He likes coffee."

The cats had slipped silently away, and Telemakos had disappeared after them. I have no idea when it happened. Only the distance of Candake's enormous knees had separated him from me, but I had never even seen him move. Candake waved a hand dismissively as the coffee things were laid before her.

"He does that all the time, artful young fox. Drives his poor grandfather to the edge of madness. How the child makes me laugh!" Which she did, violently, before lighting her burner. "His mother won't allow him coffee anyway. Now, my little queen of Sheba, set aside the mosquito Constantine while we drink together."

"Look what we found in the tax office."

I was on my way to my appointed meeting with Constantine, but he found me first, in the breezeway that connected Candake's private wing with the main body of the palace. Constantine came forward with Telemakos at his side, one hand resting on the back of the child's head. Behind them stood the impassive ceremonial spear bearers. Telemakos was still and serious, more than usually contained. He did not show it in any obvious way, but I was seeing something I had not seen in him before: he was afraid.

"Have the decency to use full grown spies in future," Constantine told me in a voice of frost.

"I have not yet stooped to spying on you," I answered in an equal tone.

Telemakos said heatedly, "I would not get caught if she did." He tilted his head back, suddenly, and winced.

Constantine had hold of his thick hair.

"Queen's pawn should be played more cautiously than this," Constantine said, and gave the child's head such a yank that Telemakos screwed his eyes shut and bared his missing teeth, though he did not make a sound.

"Here," Constantine said offhandedly, letting go and pushing the child forward with a hard smack to the back of his skull. "See him home. I may still have time for you when you get back."

It never occurred to me to acknowledge this dismissal, but Telemakos was better trained than I. He knelt before Constantine with his swift, sincere reverence and murmured, "I beg your forgiveness, my lord. I didn't know you had an appointment in the tax room."

"The last person caught hiding there was beheaded in the cathedral square," Constantine said. "It was not my office then, but I have inherited that right along with the room. It would simplify everything if I exercised it. Don't tempt me."

He blew past us, saying again in parting, "Take him home."

Telemakos and I walked through the palace gardens in silence, and through the principal gate, and started down the wide road through the wealthy suburb where Kidane's mansion lay. Along the way we met the usual salutes from the mutilated dispossessed of the war in Himyar; they waited idly in the lee of stone walls, stood close against the shade trees to avoid the rain, squatted together among the sycamores' roots to scoop out shallow cups in the damp earth and fill them with pebbles to play gebeta there. When they noticed me, they stood quietly and bowed; a few came limping in my wake. If I had been walking in the city, they would have made a crowd around me. I touched the bow at my shoulders, which I always carried when I went anywhere alone, but I did not string it. No one of the Himyar veterans had ever threatened me. I walked quickly, making Telemakos trot to keep pace with me.

"Why did the viceroy call me your pawn?"

We were almost home now. Telemakos was panting.

"Why did he—"

"He could have meant me," I said shortly. "I'm not queen yet." We both knew he had not, but Telemakos did not press me. He said instead, still panting as he tried to keep up with me and talk at the same time, "I wasn't hiding. I was stalking one of Candake's cats. I'd been following him for an hour, forever, all over the palace, and then he went to sleep in that room. I was waiting for him to wake up. I knew it was the tax office, but truly, I didn't know the viceroy had a meeting there."

I slowed my pace to match his more evenly. "What did he do when he found you?"

"One of the spear bearers found me. They search the room before he goes in. They sweep under all the furniture with their spears, and stick them in the curtains. Stop a minute, look—"

He hitched up his kilt. He had taken a long, shallow scratch up his thigh. No wonder he had been scared.

"It was an accident," Telemakos said. "Nafas did it. He was very upset."

I was guilt-stricken for having made Telemakos walk so fast, and my estimation of the emperor's silent ceremonial guards rose, as well.

I also saw that if they had accidentally killed Telemakos, Constantine would have been blameless. I saw this, and I knew that if it had happened that way, and my cousin had protested his innocence, I would never have believed him. I noted this piece of notional unfairness against Constantine as a mark against my own character. He had never lied to me, after all.

"Telemakos," I said seriously, "while Constantine is viceroy, don't run about the New Palace on your own."

"I'll be careful."

"Don't hide there. Don't stalk Candake's cats. Don't feed Caleb's monkeys."

"I play there always!"

"It's different now. Since Priamos has returned and I am here, the ministers and nobles are all suspicious of him, and me, and Constantine because I am to be married to him, and you because I stay in your house. They will check the wall hangings and palm fronds with spears and daggers. I don't want you to get hurt again."

We stood before his grandfather's gates. "Promise me this, Telemakos."

He whistled through the gap in his teeth, which he did when he was thinking.

"Can I go through the markets? And the Necropolis, where the monuments are? Can I go anywhere I like, as long as I stay out of the New Palace?"

Something occurred to me: he had said he must beg Kidane to take him to the New Palace.

"Are you usually allowed to go anywhere you like?"

"Not by myself," Telemakos said.

Suddenly I wanted him out of this. He was too obliviously innocent. If he did not serve me willingly, I would not coerce him, and he was not ready to make such choices himself.

"You can go anywhere you like," I said, "as long as someone can see you."

Telemakos answered mournfully, "That's the part I don't like. Having to stay where someone can see me. I will soon forget that part."

"Think about Nafas's spear," I told him, "and you'll not forget."

We went through the gate together. "Let's tell your mother," I added.

CHAPTER VI

✦

The Long Rains

"I WARNED YOU I should be a disagreeable guest," I uttered in a low voice. Telemakos was in bed, and Turunesh sat spinning in her private sitting room by the brilliant light of a glass oil lamp that hung from the ceiling. My own hands were idle. "I should not have allowed my quarrel with Constantine to come to this."

"Don't falter now," Turunesh said. "Hold Constantine in check. I'll take Telemakos out of it." She seemed calm as ever; her busy hands never stopped moving. "The roads are all impassable in winter, but in the new year I'll bring Telemakos to my father's country estate in Adwa."

The Aksumite new year falls in British September. It was July now; their spring was still at least six weeks away. It seemed remote and distant.

"You are too forgiving," I said, angry at myself.

"They all say that. I make a pet of my son. But he is all I

will ever have of his father, and his sweet affection melts my heart."

"It is battering away at mine, as well. I do not deserve such compassion. I am remorseless as my aunt."

"You are both kings' daughters," Turunesh agreed mildly, as though that excused even the worst excesses of libertine behavior; or indeed, as though it were reason to expect such excesses. She laid her spindle in her lap. "Princess, what other weapon do you have? I cannot condemn you. I would do the same for my kingdom, if I had to."

"All right, but *why should I have to?*"

It rained and rained. Even the doves were bad-tempered. It was worse than Britain; the rain came down torrentially, day after day. I slopped back and forth in it almost daily between Kidane's house and the New Palace, bedraggled men begging at my heels. My only consolation for making this trek was that every now and then I found Priamos left momentarily idle and able to sit and talk with me. I dragged him into the Golden Court to get him out of his room.

We sat on the marble rim of the big fountain, as we had on the morning of my arrival in the city. One of the monkeys crept up to us and climbed into Priamos's lap. Priamos fondled the elegant black-and-white creature beneath its chin, then suddenly drew taut the monkey's gold chain with one hand. Priamos said abruptly, "I hate this."

He shook the links, which rang musically. "I cannot see

any reason to keep them if they must be chained. They are supposed to be climbers and leapers."

"You said that Caleb's lions were chained."

"It made me sick to look at them." Priamos shook the monkey's lead again, and began to pick idly at the rivet that fastened it into the marble wall. "Mikael was always kept in chains," he said. "My eldest brother. When I was young, sequestered with Hector and Ityopis and Yared, we thought Mikael a terrible monster. He would shake his chains at us when we came near, just as these monkeys do. He never spoke except to recite scripture or scream for a spear. His 'serpent-slaying spear,' he called it. He is named for the saint who founded Debra Damo, and for the angel Michael."

The marble around the rivet was chipped, and Priamos worried it as he spoke. "Hector once schemed that he should furnish Mikael with a spear, just to see what he would do with it."

"What did he do with it?" I asked, fascinated.

"Nothing. Which was as well, because Hector was caught and trapped in an empty reservoir with Mikael and his serpent-slaying spear for half a week."

Priamos jerked at the monkey's chain. "I do not think often about Mikael. But I hate to see wild creatures bound. I cannot stomach it."

I remembered the cowed boy led on board the yacht in Septem, and Priamos's angry scowl, and the light, sympathetic brush of his gentle hand against mine.

Again he jerked at the golden links, and the fastening came away from the wall, bringing a spall of marble with it.

I laughed. "There, you have freed him." The elegant monkey still curled against Priamos's other arm, unaware it had been released.

Priamos set it down on the pool's rim aside of him, and laughed also. "I wonder if the rest will come away so easily," he said, and reached over me to pull at the chain on the other side of the bench. It did not.

One of his guards said politely, "Prince, best leave it—"

Priamos stood up, ignoring him. He wrapped the gold links around his hand and gave a ferocious heave, throwing all his weight against the chain. A chunk of marble the size of his fist came out of the fountain wall.

"*Hai!*"

He snatched at another chain. One guard tried to trip him with the shaft of a spear, and the other lunged for him. He was quicker than either of them. He jumped over the rim, splashed noisily across the fountain, and attacked one of the chains on the opposite side of the stone pool. The guards leaped after him, at once crying for assistance and yelling at him to stop. The monkeys already freed scampered chattering up the columns toward the coffered ceiling; those yet chained began roaring in fear or excitement.

Ityopis tore past me.

"Priamos, be not a fool!"

Priamos was fast. There were half a dozen monkeys loose

now, and there were no less than six men trying to pull him down, but Priamos seemed always to be a hairsbreadth ahead of them. Wazeb came wafting into the court as through drawn by the commotion. I could not see over all their heads, and stood on the edge of the fountain.

"Priamos, stop!" I cried in dismay, slipping unhelpfully into Latin. "Oh, God, your *hands*!" The chains were tearing them to shreds.

Ityopis caught him by one arm and struggled with him, crying out desperately, "Sir, this is madness, madness! You have waited so patiently—"

"I cannot sit here and look at them any longer," Priamos gasped, gentle Priamos, and wrenched two more monkeys free before his guards and three soldiers and a butler dragged him to the ground.

Seconds later Constantine dragged him up again by a length of his shamma, half choking him. "My God, the waste! The *expense*!" He struck Priamos viciously across the face. "Do you have any idea what it costs to keep this palace as Caleb ordered it? Or how much was thrown away on that twenty-year debacle in Himyar—"

"Seventeen," Priamos interrupted hotly. "Seventeen years it went on, not twenty."

Constantine hit him again.

"*Stop this!*" I bellowed. "You idiots both—"

"What do you know of Himyar?" Priamos blazed at Caleb's viceroy, reckless with rebellion and outrage. "What do you know of Abreha? Have you ever been there? Have you ever seen him?"

"*I know Himyar,*" Constantine said. "I was in Sana last year as Caleb's envoy, do you not remember? Abreha was so bold as to ask me to stay as his own ambassador! I know the face of treachery when I see it!"

"Well, I am not Abreha!" Priamos cried out, so impassioned he was near to weeping.

"Yet you insist on undermining my authority! You conspire with the princess who is to be my bride, you run riot in my court, and then you dare argue with me! I do not like these damned colobus any more than you do—"

"So *get rid of them!*"

Constantine struck him a third time across the face, more coldly, as though in an effort to bring him to his senses. Priamos staggered, and was held up by his guards.

"I am going to see you bound in this place as long as it takes to repair the walls," Constantine said, his voice hard and controlled. "I do not care how noble a prince you are; I will not let you test my stewardship with such brass insolence. Let everyone see what you have done."

"My lord Ella Amida," begged Ityopis, "in God's name use reason in your punishment of him."

"Am I dealing with a reasonable man? I would as soon have him flayed! Look about you!"

And the Golden Court was a ruin. Water leaked from a crack in the fountain wall where the marble had been torn out, monkeys roared and barked in the ceiling, potted trees lay uprooted and overturned, marble fragments strewed the floor.

"At least give him a choice," said Wazeb in his light, casual way.

Constantine pressed his lips together tightly; his nostrils flared. "He shall be chained here so long as it takes to mend the walls. Three days, perhaps. I do not have it in me to be gentler than this."

Priamos winced and shrank as though he had been struck again. "Three—" He swallowed, and bit at his lower lip. "Three—" Then he seemed to retch, as though the very words he tried to speak were so loathsome that he could not hold them in his mouth. "Three years or three minutes, it is all the same to me. I would sooner be flayed."

Constantine paused for a long moment, and then said levelly, "Would you?"

"Yes." Priamos answered without hesitation.

"A choice," repeated Wazeb.

Constantine sighed and glanced at Ityopis. "Just so. Ras Priamos, if you will not be bound here, then you will take a score's lash stripes on each palm. Choose."

"My God, Constantine," I cried out. "Only look at his hands!"

Priamos looked down at them himself, as if noticing for the first time the damage he had done them. He could not raise them, because the guards had hold of his arms.

"Go send for a whip," he said stubbornly.

Constantine sighed again, and nodded to the butler, who left the room. I climbed down from the pool's edge, sick at heart.

Ityopis begged fervently, "Grant the small courtesy, then, that if he takes this beating, let that be the end of it. Let this not be spoken of over and over and held as an example of his insurrection. Let it pass as an act of thoughtless passion, finished on both sides. We are all weary of the winter rains." He stopped to draw breath. "Let me see to the repairs."

"All right," said Constantine, then snorted. "The brothers Anbessa, a coalition of lions, indeed! You are a nest of scorpions."

The butler returned. He gave the whip to Constantine and asked to be dismissed.

"All right. Send for the animals keeper; we need these monkeys caught."

"Ah, let me come with you," said Wazeb. "I like the animals keeper." They left together. I stared after the boy, hating him.

"My lord Ella Amida—"

The three soldiers spoke nearly as a unit.

"Your permission to return to—"

"I should be training—"

"We are needed—"

Constantine cut them off. "I need one of you here."

The three glanced at one another. Then, by some internal decision of their own, one of them stepped forward determinedly and took the whip from Constantine. The other two soldiers turned and saluted Priamos on their way out.

Ityopis said politely, "You do not need an audience, lord," and turned on his heel also.

"Ras Priamos," said Constantine.

Priamos knelt between his guards. His lip was bleeding. He held out one hand, palm up, as though holding something precious and invisible in its cup: as he had held out his hand to me when he offered me my passage to Aksum.

"Peace to you, Priamos Anbessa," I said levelly in Ethiopic, and followed Ityopis.

I heard the first swish and crack before I had left the Golden Court. Abandoning dignity, I fled with my hands over my ears before I heard anything more.

Ityopis was ahead of me, shuddering in the corridor. He turned to me and offered me his arm: peacemaker, Priamos had called him.

"I stand amazed that martinet finds any man ready to administer his punishments," he gasped. "Half the soldiers in this city fought under my brother in Himyar. They'd cut out their own hearts to spare him. Mother of God, to threaten him with chains! Constantine can have no idea what it is to begin life on Debra Damo. Any one of us would have chosen as Priamos did, given such choices."

"Priamos told me of Mikael's chains," I said.

"Mikael's chains!" Ityopis gave a hoarse bark of laughter, like a cough. "Mikael's! Ai! And did he tell you of his own? How he and Hector were fettered back to back for four nights, the time they got a spear for Mikael? Four nights they lay in a pit with the madman. They took it in turns sleeping so they might constantly watch him; they nearly skinned themselves trying to break free. Priamos still carries the marks left by the irons."

Ityopis's words struck me like a blow to the chest, stopping my breath. Priamos had given me no hint that he had taken part in Hector's scheme.

"He speaks with all the careful government of a rock slide," Ityopis uttered bitterly. "'Go send for a whip'! Small wonder our mother names him hornbill."

Constantine came storming out of the Golden Court.

"Let us talk for a minute, Goewin."

He pulled my arm away from its link with Ityopis's elbow, and took me roughly by my wrists. He held my hands up, imprisoned, as he spoke. I was nearly as tall as he, but I was not as strong. And I would not humiliate myself by struggling with him. I stood struck with frost, unmoving and unyielding.

"Explain a thing to the princess for me, Ras Ityopis," Constantine said coldly. "She has more Ethiopic than any of us guess. Tell her about the behavior of coalition lions."

Ityopis protested in a low voice, "My lord, I do not understand—"

"Explain to her why the brothers Anbessa are named a coalition."

I stood between them in the hall, held captive in Constantine's hard grip, while Ityopis reluctantly obeyed the viceroy's order and explained to me the social habits of lions.

"Male lions form lifelong allegiances. Not with their mates, but with one another. They may leave a pride, they may leave their lionesses and cubs, or a rival coalition may send them off. But an allied group of males stays together, and hunts together, and fights together. Coalition lions will defend their comrades to the death. They are more faithful to the members of their coalition than to their mates or their kits."

"You have not yet explained the brothers Anbessa," Constantine reminded him.

Ityopis swallowed. "We are a coalition of lions," he said in a low voice, "because it is said that any one of us will defend another to the death, as do brotherhood lions. Sir," he said, turning to Constantine with his head bowed, "my lord, Abreha was never one of us. He is seventeen years my senior. Priamos had never laid eyes on him until the carnage at al-Muza. Abreha is not—"

"He slew the emperor Caleb's eldest son, but he set Priamos free unscathed. When a coalition takes over a pride, they drive out the existing coalition and kill their cubs."

Ityopis dared to protest, "Priamos is not Abreha!"

"You, Ras Ityopis, you tread a very narrow path, and my ministers and I can find no fault in you. But Priamos—"

Constantine dug his nails into my wrists. I clenched my teeth and did not flinch.

"You did not want to see him whipped," he said to me softly.

"No one did! Even your young imperial catspaw, even Wazeb made an excuse!"

"Now listen, Goewin: I will not have you inciting Priamos again."

"God help me, I won't," I swore ardently.

"You will not. I will see to it. I will provide you with a guard. They will stay with you here in the New Palace, and ensure you do not come anywhere near him." He paused. "You'll be thankful to find an imperial escort waiting for you in the street when you venture out alone; you will keep out of harm's way as well as out of trouble. You will not need protection within the walls of Kidane's villa, of course, but it will be pleasant for you to be able to walk about the city without fearing a ragged flock of Himyar veterans begging at your heels."

This was entirely within his jurisdiction. I bit down hard on the protests that rose in my throat, and said only, in a voice like ice:

"If I may take a hostage, so may you."

"You are my betrothed, not my hostage," said Constantine. "And Wazeb is my ward. It is Priamos who is my catspaw. Cross me again, Goewin, and I swear I will find a way to use it against him."

He dropped my wrists, at last, disdainfully.

"Lij Telemakos Meder, heir to the house of Nebir; Ras Priamos Anbessa, heir to the house of Lazen. How many more will you place in jeopardy? Your proud will may soon determine the fate of half the Aksumite imperial court," he commented, and blew angrily on his way.

CHAPTER VII

✹

Prisoners

I DREAMED I was trapped in a deep well full of chained lions, and I watched Telemakos free them one by one as he pulled their iron chains out of the stone walls. Don't do that, I kept telling him, and he answered: I'm not afraid of lions. Blood flew from his golden fingers like drops of water. I woke all Kidane's household, screeching.

I dreamed the Golden Court was littered with broken glass in gleaming colors, like the shards with which Lleu had once mended the mosaic floors of our villa at Camlan. Priamos chased lion cubs over the bright slivers on bleeding feet, while I apologized to Constantine for the stained floor.

I dreaded sleep. I sat late in Turunesh's sitting room, listening to the running gutters, reading by the ethereal light of her glass ceiling lamp.

The young men who protected me in the street were shy and quiet, serious and disciplined. Constantine never sent the same collection two days running. I was hard pressed to learn any of their names; they would not look at me. They stared straight beyond me as we marched together through Aksum's plazas and markets, their spears bristling, daring anyone to come near. There was always a group of four waiting for me outside Kidane's gate, an imposing group of handsome spearmen. Passersby stared. I did not like to make a spectacle of my hosts.

Kidane's mild comment was: "Our first British ambassador was a more subtle suitor."

"He was as persistent," said Turunesh.

When I tried to climb the grand stairway leading to the upper stories of the New Palace where Priamos was kept prisoner, I met with the same blank-faced, apologetic guards that waited for me in the street.

"Remember me to Ras Priamos," I said to them, feeling both furious and pathetic. I said it also many times to Halen, and Ityopis, and Candake; and once, in desperation, I sent Telemakos as my message bearer, and suffered a punishing few hours of frantic guilt and worry while Telemakos took advantage of this unanticipated release from his own bondage. I never saw Priamos myself, no matter where I went.

And this went on for weeks.

Winter was drawing to an end. The rain grew less constant, then erratic, then stopped altogether. It was September, the Aksumite new year, and the sloping fields around the city exploded in a blaze of golden asters.

"Would you like to come to Adwa with us?" Turunesh asked me, scattering grain across the flagged courtyard for the doves. She and Telemakos fed them together, ritually, before he went to bed.

"Not with the imperial guard trotting at my heels," I answered.

Turunesh said calmly, "We can get you out of the city in secret. We can take you out through the Necropolis. There is a tunnel from this house to the family vault, for use in funerals."

The Necropolis spread vast and silent on the slopes beyond the cathedral, an imposing cemetery of towering monoliths and stately mausoleums. The tall stelae stood over the graves of ancient Aksumite kings.

"A tunnel from this house?" I repeated quietly. "What can you mean?"

"The ground beneath the city is a warren of tunnels," Telemakos said, trying to tease a dove out of its niche and into his hands. "One of them stretches from here to Kolöe."

"You do hear the most improbable things!" Turunesh exclaimed. "It is upward of eighty miles to Kolöe. Our own passage leads only to the tomb of the house of Nebir, but that is a good distance across the city."

"She used to play in it with her cousins," Telemakos said. "The tunnel, I mean, not the tomb."

"It is an accursed struggle keeping the boy out of it."

Telemakos cupped his hands together to coo and warble through them, and ignored his mother.

"Could I really get through without anyone knowing?" I asked.

"We would have to lead you to the vault and then go back through the house while you waited for us to let you out on the other side."

"What would I do in Adwa, though?" I paced to the fishpond and back. "I'd be free of Constantine's guard, at any rate." A wild thought occurred to me. "I could go to Abreha. He wants his own British ambassador in Himyar, Constantine said."

"Or you might seek out Caleb," Turunesh suggested softly. "When he passes his golden head cloth to Wazeb, Ella Amida's authority will end."

"Is that what happens?"

"That is what Caleb said would happen, before he left. But he did not tell anyone where he was going, or if he would return. People say he's in the monastery Abba Pantelewon, above the city here. Though at the same time they say he has gone to the mountain of Ophar in the Salt Desert."

Telemakos lowered his cupped hands. "He's in Debra Damo," he said, and pressed his cheek against the granite by the pigeonhole, warm with the setting sun. "Do come out, Creamy, I have honey water here for good little doves—"

I stared at the child. Turunesh caught him by the shoulder and made him turn around to face us.

"Where did you hear that?"

"Candake said it, do you not remember, Goewin? She said that Caleb would retire to the dragon's hermitage while Ella Amida patched up his empire. That is Debra Damo, isn't it?

In Ras Priamos's book of maps there is a picture of a dragon guarding it."

"Is there nothing that escapes your attention?" Turunesh gave her son's shoulder an abrupt shake and let go of him. Then she sighed and absently threw another handful of grain for the birds at our feet.

I said in wonder, "Might Caleb have gone to Debra Damo?"

"He might indeed," Turunesh answered. "He has been there before. He took Medraut to visit there."

She reached out to touch my hand. "If Caleb is in Debra Damo—he would pardon Priamos. And he would see to Telemakos's safety himself, I know it. He would do it for Medraut." She did not take her eyes off Telemakos. "They do not allow women in the monastery, but we could take the boy to be our messenger."

"Are you sure Candake meant Debra Damo?"

"We can ask her," Turunesh said. She knelt by Telemakos and said gently at his ear, "Shall we take up Candake's invitation to join her at the Feast of the Cross?"

So Turunesh and Telemakos and I sat with Candake throughout the endless Meskal ceremony in the cathedral square, while the courtiers and soldiers of the Aksumite court pledged another year's service to their empire.

Constantine greeted me most civilly when we arrived, before the formalities began. I am sure he was feeling more smug than he allowed himself to behave, seeing me and my hosts well-guarded.

"The rains are over," he said, "and in a few months the winds will change. You will be able to go home soon, my cousin. I pray that you will take me with you, and not some lesser instrument."

"What will you do with the regency here?"

"I have arranged that Danael will become viceroy. I cannot turn over the kingship to Wazeb while his father lives, without his father's blessing; Caleb has forbidden it."

Then he turned to respond to some other minister, and Turunesh and I sought Candake. I knew Constantine would not speak to me again that day. He avoided the queen of queens.

Candake had her own stand, close to the thrones of the viceroy and the emperor-in-waiting, but clearly separate from them. She bellowed a greeting to us and banned my guards with her own. They laughed and saluted one another as she ordered us to sit beneath her fringed umbrellas of green and scarlet silk, and set about feeding us fried cakes.

Candake explained for us, loudly, every detail of the parade.

"Those are the officers who lead the fleet. That is Anda, a very nasty man; he has charge of the Arabian prisoners who toil in the northern gold mines. HOW MANY HAVE YOU SLAIN THIS YEAR, ANDA?"

No one dared laugh at her, or shut her up.

"Those squadrons patrol the Highway of the Cataracts.

Those with the arrows on their helms patrol the lands of the Beja, where emeralds come from."

She knew everyone; she knew everything. Hours passed, and she did not fail to identify a single officer. She fed us so much that Telemakos was sick. As the day wore on and his wild excitement began to reshape itself into wild boredom, she taught him finger games and made her attendants arrange his arms and legs and chair as they arranged hers. She was the only one of us who did not flag in her enthusiasm for the spectacle, and the only one of us who seemed to remain in perfect humor. Telemakos finally fell asleep with his head in her enormous lap.

"His hair is not so silken as yours, is it, Goewin, little Sheba? But such a color, like the snow of the Simien Mountains! Your brother let me put his own icy hair into plaits once. He looked like a gorgon."

She sighed, and smoothed a hand over Telemakos's head. Then she gave another chuckle.

"There are the bala heg at last. When they have finished, we can go home. The afa negus must take his turn before them, though. HALEN, you let my son speak FIRST."

At her sudden shout, Telemakos raised his head with a jerk and stared at the parade. There, alongside his tutor, was Priamos. When Candake called out to the afa negus, they both looked across at us. Priamos made a bow to his mother, and saluted me like a soldier. He must have been no more than ten feet away from me as he knelt before Wazeb. It was the first I had seen him in nearly six weeks.

"Goewin, Goewin," said Telemakos, pulling at my elbow, "you are crying! Look, my lady queen, you've made her weep, shouting like that."

"It's the sun," I snapped at him.

Turunesh took hold of his hands and held him close against her. She whispered at his ear, "Hush, my love. This is a solemn ritual now. Not another word from you till it is over. Only listen."

Candake, in her single minute's silence of the afternoon, listened as Priamos renewed his vows of service to his sovereign and state, first to Wazeb and then to Constantine.

"Hum," she grunted, when he had finished. "Men! They come and go, they snatch at power, they wander off to beat each other over the head. But I stay in one place, and they all come back to me: brothers, nephews, sons. The lioness is the pride's heart, not the coalition."

Priamos joined the ranks of other officers across the square. He was guarded even now. He did not dare to look at me again.

"Is he well?" I asked.

"Aye, as may be, girl," Candake said darkly. "As may be. Losing his temper last month did him no great service."

I watched him standing quiet and calm across the square.

"The best of my sons, he is," Candake wheezed, but for once she did not laugh. "The best of my sons. Do you hear that, ITYOPIS, you POMPOUS YOUNG LICKER OF ROYAL BOOTS? The best of you all, Priamos is. You might have stopped it—"

She stopped screaming. Ityopis stood cringing as he waited his turn in the parade, and so did Priamos, both looking as though they hoped the underground tunnels would kindly open and swallow them.

"You might have stopped it, too, Goewin dragon's daughter," Candake said in a normal voice, rocking as though she were chanting. "There was no need for him to be punished like a drunkard in the marketplace. For loosing ten monkeys! He came to eat with me a day after the beating, and his hands were still so swollen he could not feed himself. He sat and wept into his coffee as I have not seen him weep since the night he came back from the Himyar."

"Candake," I said slowly, "you will kill me if you go on."

"You did not have to endure it."

"I am enduring it now." I clenched my teeth. "I know, I know it is my fault. I cannot sleep, knowing I have brought him to such disgrace."

Candake shifted her weight and consoled herself with another three fried cakes, and then said wearily, "Go home, girl. Go home and take your bridegroom the mosquito with you, as you intended."

"I hate my bridegroom the mosquito," I said vehemently, heedless of who might hear. "How I detest him! To threaten a child of six summers with beheading!"

Turunesh gazed serenely at the solemn procession of ministers, as each knelt and spoke in turn. She held Telemakos tight and still against her side.

"Constantine keeps me prisoner, I can barely speak to him civilly; I do not know why he should ever want to complete our union."

"Because you are beautiful," Candake said.

Telemakos was watching me, not the ceremony.

"'Fair as the moon, bright as the sun, terrible as an army with banners.'" Candake wheezed again as she settled herself more comfortably. "So sings Solomon to Sheba in the Song of Songs. You cannot see yourself! 'Terrible as an army with banners.' How should dogged Constantine court such majesty? His promised bride is beyond his grasp, and he is eaten up with jealousy."

"What do you mean?"

"Silly girl, why do you think he deals so harshly with my gentle son?" she said sadly. "The mosquito is eaten up with envy because Priamos, though he has never courted kingship, has courted you, and owns your heart."

I opened my mouth to protest that no man should ever own my heart or any part of me. No words came. All I could produce was a small, quiet spate of bewildering tears, which I swiped at angrily. I stared across the square at Priamos Anbessa.

So he does, I realized. So he does.

"He *wept* when they told him you were no longer allowed to see him. He WEPT. How much weeping have you done on his account, girl?"

"I wake up screaming every night on his account," I said

fiercely, and scrubbed at my eyes. "My God! What hope is there for either of us?"

"Go home, girl." Candake closed her eyes, as though she were so tired of it all. "I do not want my wise and noble son to spend his life prisoner to a mosquito."

"I will not leave Aksum until I see Ras Priamos go free," I said through my teeth.

"He will never go free while you are here."

Ityopis had made his pledge, and Kidane. Danael was finishing his. I took Candake's hand, leaned in over her enormous bulk, and kissed her painted cheek.

She was more like my aunt Morgause than I had realized. Not in that she was cruel, for she was not; but in that for all her loud and acrid talk she was without authority, she was helpless. Her sons' fate was utterly beyond her control. She could not even walk without assistance.

I said at her ear, "Dear lady, Queen of Queens. Might not your brother's word override my cousin's? Or the emperor's override the viceroy's? If you will tell me where to find him, I will seek out Caleb instead of going home, and bring your nephew his golden head cloth."

Candake sighed. She traced the track of a tear across my cheek with a large, soft fingertip, and sighed again.

"Ah, proud little Sheba," she said. "Nor should you be made to spend your life prisoner to a mosquito, either."

PART
III

FLIGHT

CHAPTER VIII

✦

The Tomb of the False Door

WAZEB PAID A visit to Kidane's mansion, a day later. He came with his own retinue, which he left at the gate along with Constantine's escort for me, so that it looked as though there were rival factions preparing for a small battle on Kidane's doorstep. Wazeb wore his customary simple white cotton kilt and head cloth bound with grass, though on this occasion the ends of his shamma were pinned with a great clasp of gold and emerald.

He came upstairs to share imported wine with us, to the joy and terror of Kidane's servants. He had a disconcerting habit of rewarding the attendant women by feeding them sweets out of his hand. He was most at ease in Kidane's house.

"Have you heard any of our old stories?" he asked me. "Will you understand if I speak in my own language?"

"Please do. I'll try."

"I have a favorite story. It is of Menelik, the queen of Sheba's son, and tells of his visit to Solomon, his father. When

Menelik returns to his mother, he steals the Ark of the Covenant from Solomon. And Solomon discovers him. But instead of punishing him, Solomon gives him the Ark and lets him go free."

Wazeb stopped speaking for a moment, and everyone in the room waited in expectant silence.

"Solomon is remembered for his wisdom," Wazeb said. "But when I am shown his likeness in the pictures, I do not make note of his wisdom. It is the face of forgiveness that I see in him."

He raised his head a little, proudly. It would be another year and more before his beard began to grow.

"I should like to be wise enough to grant forgiveness," he said, "like Solomon; like Christ."

I nodded, slowly, staring at him. I had not got in the habit of lowering my eyes in the presence of authority, and as the emperor's heir, neither had he; so when he raised his head, for a moment we looked into each other's eyes.

"When I am emperor, I will take the name Gebre Meskal," he said. "The servant of the cross."

"You have noble ambitions," I said, thinking to glance away, then astonished that I had done so.

Wazeb beckoned to his footman. "My aunt Candake sends you a present, Princess Goewin," he said in lighter tones. "She knows you have trouble sleeping, and is so kind to give you a book to read. She thinks you will like this. Your nephew told her you like maps."

He put into my hands Priamos's *Red Sea Itinerary*.

"The queen of queens tells you to study these," said Wazeb. "She thinks you will find them entertaining. Here, let me show you."

He turned the pages carefully until he came to the stylized church on the cliff, with the dragon at its foot.

"Here is one. This shows you the road to the hermitage at Debra Damo, among the amba plateaus, where the emperor's nephews are sequestered."

"How did the queen of queens come by this book?"

"It was a gift," Wazeb answered blandly. "Look, here are marked all the villages along the way, and the distances between them. Even the turnings are numbered."

And so they were, in Greek and Latin.

The Greek notations had been made by the artist who drew the pictures, the script small and elegant. But the Latin translations had been written out by another hand, in bold, straight, careful capitals like an inscription on a monument, as though the writer were not entirely at ease with an unfamiliar set of letters. The last in the list of names and numbers was "Solomon VIII XIV." It did not appear in the Greek text, but only in the scrupulous Latin.

"This is not a turning, is it?" I said slowly. "This name Solomon, and these figures?"

Wazeb laughed. "It is more likely a biblical text. Though I do not know why it is marked here."

"Can you tell me the text?"

"'Make haste, my beloved.'"

I stared at the page, then raised my eyes to look at Wazeb.

He chanted softly, with his serene smile. "'Make haste, my beloved, and be like a gazelle or a young stag upon the mountains of spices.'

"It is the end of the Song of Songs," he said. "Solomon to Sheba, perhaps." He bent over the book again, and remarked, "The writing is very fine."

"It's beautiful," I said.

Turunesh unlocked a door in one of the recesses at the base of Kidane's house. It was night, and we moved without a light. Telemakos squeezed my hand in fits and starts, presumably because his mother's hands were busy and it was the only thing he could do to keep himself from hopping from foot to foot in giddy excitement.

None of us spoke until Turunesh had closed the door behind us and lit an earthen lamp. We stood on a narrow landing; a steep stair led below the house. The walls were laid with the same granite blocks as the house itself until halfway down the stair, and from there the way was cut into solid rock.

Turunesh passed the lamp to me and drew Telemakos close against her.

"Now listen, my hero. You are to obey the princess as you would obey me. As you would obey Grandfather. You will have to wait for me at the other end, and it will be dark, and maybe days before I am able to let you through."

"I'm not afraid of the dark," Telemakos said, fearless and careless, just the way he said in my dreams, I'm not afraid of lions.

Turunesh lit our way with the oil lamp and carried a bag of food over her shoulder; I carried water flasks, blankets, and my bow. Telemakos carried his own small canvas satchel. The tunnel was narrow, but clean and bare and dry. You could not have guessed where it led, or why it was there.

"How old is this?" I asked.

"Not very old. A hundred and fifty years, perhaps. Our house is older. The tunnel was built when the new family tomb was built, to connect them. Look, here is one of the older passages. The city is riddled with them."

She put a shielding hand over the flaming wick of her lamps as we passed a low opening in one of the walls.

Our passage turned twice, and crossed five other ways, but generally it was straight. It sloped gently downward for perhaps three quarters of a mile to a wooden door. Past this, Turunesh led us up another stair and through a hall whose arched ceiling was laid with brick. We came at last to a wide chamber where the floor was a ledge of stone slabs surrounding a flight of steps leading into darkness below. Halfway up the wall across the pit was another door, this one cut into solid granite and set between stone lintels.

"It's false," said Turunesh. "Even the hasp, carved into the stone. It's the door to the spirit world. This court used to be open to the sky; my grandparents sealed it not long after my father was born. The stairway to the left leads you out. We will put the lamp out now, because the chamber below this level is built so that it draws in winds that suddenly quench a burning flame."

She raised the lamp to her lips to blow it out.

Telemakos cried out softly, "Oh, Mother, bring the light down so we can watch the wind put it out!"

"You mad creature," she laughed. "All right. I'll hold the light; you and the princess go down first."

It was dim even with the light above us. Telemakos and I crept down the stairs, brushing the wall with our fingertips. We stood at the bottom and watched Turunesh make her careful descent; you could feel the sudden winds—light, gently rippling over the back of your neck. Turunesh's lamp winked out without warning.

"You can be sure my cousins and I nearly died of fright when first this tunnel blew our lights out," came her calm voice out of the dark.

Telemakos laughed.

"Hold the lamp and I'll hold your hand, child. Princess, take my other hand."

Her hands were steady. We walked forward in the darkness.

The true entrance to the tomb of the false door was sealed with an iron lock. Telemakos leaned against my waist while Turunesh unfastened the lock and opened the stone door. A smell of herbs and damp earth hit us. It was not a foul smell, but a strange smell to find in the still air of the stone underground.

"No one will come here," Turunesh said. "The vaults are locked against robbers, and the cemetery is patrolled aboveground. I will have to bribe the warden, I think, before I will get in to you from the other side."

"Do you mean for us to shut ourselves in the vault?" I said, as lightly as I could.

"Stay in the corridor unless you need to hide. I can't believe anyone will come down here, but all the wealthy villas have access to these tunnels, and I don't know who else. The door to the vault will not open from the inside, though, so do not shut yourself in unless you are very frightened. Will you be all right without a light? You will have no means to keep one aflame in this corridor."

I sensed her moving close to me and felt her brush against my skirt as she took her son in her arms. She whispered something at his ear, and he laughed again.

Turunesh stood, and reached for my hand one last time. "Princess, all will be well. Our household will soon discover you missing, but Ferem knows you are with me and will keep them hushed. I packed the boy's nurse off to visit her mother. There is no one else who could guess."

"Wazeb," I said. "He brought the map."

"I think the tame lion is something more than message bearer in this intrigue," Turunesh said carefully. "I think he would sooner cast dust on your trail than send dogs after you.

He has reason to hope you succeed in your quest. He awaits the advent of his own kingship. He knows what he is doing."

Turunesh squeezed my hand a final time.

"'Love is strong as death,'" she said. "'Jealousy is cruel as the grave.' If I cannot leave you light, I leave you the Song of Songs."

She went away up the stairs. For a moment we watched the glow as she lit her lamp in the upper hall, and then it was dark again.

Telemakos did not allow me to brood. He rummaged in the food bag and chattered and demanded that I tell him stories. He had invented a game, remember? Where you traced a picture of an animal in the palm of the other person's hand and tried to guess what it was. He was astonishingly good at this, his invisible sketches quick and simple, focused on the most important characteristics of a thing: whiskers, fins, wings; a giraffe's long neck; an elephant's long nose; a lion's mane.

He was good at guessing, too. I bent over his hand and drew a strange shape there.

"Winged serpent," he said immediately. "Cheater. That's not a real animal. What's this—"

His design lost me in its complexity. "I give up."

"Map of the world."

I burst out laughing.

Eventually Telemakos fell asleep, suddenly sagging against my side in the middle of a story. I folded a blanket over his small shoulders, and over my lap. I slept well when I slept at last.

But I woke suddenly with the strongest, strangest sense of loss and betrayal I have ever felt. It was like the lingering of a nightmare, except I had not been dreaming, that I could remember. I sat up in the dark.

"Telemakos?"

There was no light at all. He had been sleeping with his head in my lap, but he was not there now. I brushed my hands blindly over the cool stone on either side of me.

"Telemakos!" I hissed. I did not dare to shout. Suddenly I did not like the sound of my voice in that still, closed place.

He was gone.

A *warren of tunnels*, he had said. One of them was supposed to lead to a city eighty miles away. Where in blazes had he gone—I did not even have a light. If I set out after him, we would both be lost.

"Telemakos!" I called in panic.

I called and called, softly, as I had called hopelessly to his father in the caves of Elder Field, half a year and half the world away. The memory of it was so vivid that for a time I did not know where I was. I stood again deep in the high king's copper mines, my family lying still and shrouded at my back, calling and calling my brother's name into the unanswering earth.

I cannot, *I cannot* be doing this again. I cannot lose my brother and his son in the same insane way—

I called Telemakos for an hour, perhaps; who knows how long. Then I threw myself on the floor in despair and cried until I could not breathe.

He came back, of course. I did not hear him or know he was there until he touched me, reaching out a hand lightly to make certain where I was, then locking his small arms around my neck affectionately.

"Goewin, Goewin! What happened? Why are you crying so hard?"

"You miserable sneaking little weasel!" I gasped, hugging him against me so fiercely that he choked, and tried to break free. "Pestilent son of a demon! Where have you been all this time? How did you find your way back? Good God, how you've frightened me!"

"I'm not so stupid," he said defensively, and put into my hands a bobbin of his mother's spinning, half filled with fine wool thread.

"You came prepared," I spat through my teeth. "What if the line had broken?"

"It's quite strong," came his clear, confident voice in the dark; "try it."

I tugged at a length of wool. He was right.

"Anyway, I could smell where our camp is. The tomb's got such a different air to the tunnels; and Mother packed raisin cakes for us."

"Give me your hand," I said firmly.

I found it in the dark, offered willingly. I looped the thread around his wrist, three times, five times, a dozen times.

"What are you doing?" he whispered.

"Binding you to me," I said sharply, pulling the knots tight and beginning to loop the thread around my own hand as well.

"Do not—"

He tried to pull his hand away, too late; I held him fast.

"I won't leave you again, I promise!"

"You will not. I will see to it."

Our wrists were back to back now, webbed in wool floss.

"Is that too tight?"

"I'm all right," Telemakos answered meekly. But instead of trying to pull away again, he curled himself against my side in the dark and finally whispered, "I'm sorry, my lady."

We had no way of telling the hour. I tried to make Telemakos eat and drink sparingly. Keeping him tied to me began to prove unimaginably awkward, but I would sooner have been stripped and flogged in the cathedral square than I would have let him go again.

We were asleep when Turunesh came for us.

"Let's go," she said in urgent Ethiopic. She repeated the command in Greek, and then in Latin. "Let's go, let us go, let us go. My father is growing suspicious, wondering why he has not seen you. I don't want to compromise his standing in the Council, or with Ella Amida; better he worry, knowing nothing, than be cast as a collaborator. Ai, this is proving more difficult than I thought. I had a time persuading the gatekeeper to let me in the cemetery so late at night."

She closed the door of the tomb and fastened it, moving with sure efficiency in the dark. Then she tried to take my hand.

"Mercy on us, what is this?"

She plucked at the wool that bound Telemakos's wrist to mine.

"Your son decided to go exploring," I uttered through tight lips.

"Ai, you wretched child!" she exclaimed. "I'll have you whipped! This is not a game!"

Briefly, Turunesh tried to unpick the knots, but she quickly dropped our hands and gave up. "What a tangle! Come up out of the dark and we'll cut you apart."

Turunesh steered us around like a team of oxen, and set us walking ahead of her up the stairs. I could hear her hand brushing lightly upon the walls behind me as she felt her way. "We are nearly there," she said. "I will not make a light; it will only blind us and hurt your eyes. I've horses waiting for us at the reservoir at Mai Shum. I hope; I left them unguarded. We must reach Adwa tonight and be away to the east tomorrow. Were you able to sleep?"

"A little. How long has it been since you left us?"

"Just more than a day. Look, the far stairway. You see the stars where the door stands open at the top?"

We came out into the cemetery. The moonless night was alluringly beautiful; the spangled sky seemed like the brightest thing I had ever seen. The city below the Necropolis glittered also. I could make out the pattern of the lighted streets in the market area, where people still shopped and sold by the light of oil lamps and torches. Turunesh led us to a decorative arbor, and we sat in its shelter on a marble bench overlooking the sparkling city. She dug in her satchel and finally produced a flint fire-lighter.

"I haven't a knife. This will have to do."

When the wool cord was pulled taut beneath the flint, it seemed to grow razor-sharp, and Telemakos screwed his eyes shut and turned his face away, silent and cowed, as his mother and I took turns at sawing us free.

"Maybe we won't have you whipped after all," she said at last, with sympathy, when finally Telemakos and I were parted from each other. "Remind me to take a knife with us when we leave Adwa."

Telemakos began rather desperately to pull the frayed and tangled threads away from his wrist.

"Don't drop those on the ground," Turunesh warned. "I don't want to leave tracks."

She put the flint away and produced an earthen flask stoppered with cork.

"Have some coffee," she said. Telemakos glanced up at her then with a hopeful half-smile, rallying. "It should be hot still. Some punishment, eh? This is no precedent, boy, don't expect more tomorrow. But you need to wake properly, if we are to start."

The three of us shared the bitter drink in the dark,

beneath the shadow of the carved monuments to kings long dead.

"Will we be followed, do you think?" I asked.

"No one is hunting, yet," Turunesh answered. "The gate-keeper to the Necropolis thinks I have arranged a lover's tryst here tonight! He will pretend not to see us coming and going. You look a little like a boy with your head wrapped in a tur-ban. Tie your shamma so, and bind your skirts at the knee. The bow you carry will help fool him, as well; you will seem to be what he expects to see. Give your bundles to the child, so he may be taken as your porter."

We looked at Telemakos, quietly sipping his coffee, and relishing it. His hair caught the starlight.

Turunesh sighed. "Have you another scarf, Princess?" she said. "Half the city will recognize him if we don't hide his hair."

Telemakos looked up.

"You don't need to hide my hair," he said. "No one will see me."

"What do you mean, boy?"

His incomplete smile suddenly reminded me of his father.

"Let me go ahead on my own. I'll meet you at Mai Shum," he said. "I promise."

Turunesh threw up her hands in baffled despair, but I nod-ded in agreement.

"Trust him," I said. "No one will see him, and he won't get lost."

Telemakos stood up, pulled his satchel strap over his head,

and handed me the bag. Then he took off his shamma, folded it carefully, and laid it in his mother's lap.

"It gets in my way," he explained, his hands resting on the cloth in her lap.

"Take care, love," Turunesh said softly.

Telemakos did not answer. He leaned close to his mother to touch his cheek to hers and kissed her, then turned away and cantered lightly down the hill toward the gate. We saw him go, but we did not hear him. He did not make a sound.

CHAPTER IX

❖

Lord of the Land

TELEMAKOS WAS WAITING for us with the horses. He was there ahead of us, as he had promised. He rode with me, before me in the saddle, and none of us ever said anything more about the tunnels.

We left the city of Aksum. We followed the graveled high road to Adwa, three hours' journey under the thick and luminous stars. We reached Kidane's country estate in time to sleep before the sun rose, but we did not dare remain throughout the day. We were still close enough to Aksum that we could easily be tracked. We studied the *Itinerary* over our hasty breakfast.

"There are two ways to go," I said. "One of them looks twice the distance, but the other follows the main road. If we take the longer route we can leave the highway today."

"Good," said Turunesh. "Your white face will be remarked by everyone who passes you."

We took one of the farm ponies for Telemakos and set out.

The roadside sparked with the wild gold of Meskal daisies, the bright asters of the Aksumite highlands. Terraced fields sloped toward woodland where coffee grew wild and monkeys danced across the treetops.

"I want to see lions," Telemakos said.

"I don't!" his mother exclaimed. "What shall we do if we come by a pack of lionesses hunting, hope the princess has enough arrows in her quiver to take them all herself?"

"Maybe she could. She is Ras Meder's sister, and he could. His name was lion."

"Medraut means marksman," I said abruptly, "not lion."

"The lion is lord of the land. Meder. It doesn't mean lion, but it *is*." Telemakos spoke with absolute conviction; of course, it was his own name, as well.

"Where do you hear such things?" his mother asked mildly.

He tilted his head. "I hear everything."

We slept through the heat of the day in the village at Hawelti, then came through the trees at night. We saw nothing of the forest, but it breathed with rustling night birds and the cries of foxes and hyenas. The strange hours we were keeping put Telemakos in a fey temper. Turuncsh worried constantly about attack from wild beasts. Once we were beyond easy reach of Aksum we stopped traveling by night.

Soon the road coiled around mountain peaks that marched endlessly away from us on all sides. The air grew rarer, and now that we were well beyond the merchant ways, the road was no longer well maintained. The recent rains had done it no good either, and in one place it was so badly damaged that there were ruts in it up to Telemakos's chest. Country children wearing crosses of woven grass, like Wazeb's, helped lead us through the worst sections of the trail. Their parents offered us fried bread and handfuls of spiced, roasted grain. Everyone we met was fascinated by Telemakos, more so even than by me.

"Foreigner! Foreign ones!" they cried in greeting. Telemakos got called also "salt-top" and something that might have meant "milkman," presumably on account of his white hair.

"I am Aksumite!" he yelled back at them, or if he was feeling particularly insulted, "Bushpig herders!"

At last the rocky tablelands of the amba plateaus rose ahead of us. We could see the amba Debra Damo days before we arrived there, as we made our way through the ravines and rocky valleys.

"Are we going to stay with the monks?" Telemakos asked. "Will we worship in a church cut from rock?"

"We will stay in the pilgrims' quarters at the foot of the cliff," Turunesh said. "Do not pull at your pony's mane like that; she is tired, too."

We had left the mountain villages behind. We traveled through desolate country for hours and saw no one. Then, three days' journey from our destination, we picked up an escort.

A young man and a herd of goats joined us. The goatherd greeted us politely and kept a discreet distance, walking well behind; and we thought nothing of it when by and by we came across another goatherd. The two men spoke quietly to each other, as though they had arranged to meet, and then each turned back the way he had come. So now we traveled with a different man. He stayed with us through the afternoon; then he, too, went his way, so that we were alone, or thought we were alone, for the night. In the morning two new travelers joined us.

These were dressed in white robes bordered with broad red stripes, priests' robes, except the men seemed young for priests. They carried bows and hunting knives. They made a great show of binding their knives in their sheaths so that they might travel with us. In the middle of the day they left us, and later we found ourselves in the company of two like them, but not the same.

Then I decided that someone must have been watching and following us well before we became aware of it. The road to Debra Damo was patrolled for fifty miles. No one challenged our right to use that road or showed any interest in our destination. But we were guarded ever more constantly as we came closer to the hermitage.

At the bottom of the amba was a small settlement, and two matronly women guided us to the cluster of huts that were kept ready for pilgrims. They spoke to us with frank and friendly interest.

"They will not let you in, you know. It is a solemnly kept man's community; they do not even keep nanny goats."

"The boy will act as our messenger," Turunesh said calmly.

"Is he to be dedicated? If you are of the house of Nebir,

you may sequester him here with the children of the queen of queens," one of them offered helpfully.

The other gave Telemakos a sharp look and said to her companion, "His house is of no account. You can see why they would bring him here."

They both stopped still in their tracks and gazed at Telemakos.

"I see, I see," said the first.

Telemakos scowled but held his tongue. He rubbed at his wrist where I had bound him, though it could not possibly bother him anymore.

It made me think of Priamos rubbing at his own wrist in the exact same way, rubbing away the ghost of a chain. Priamos had been even younger than Telemakos when he came to Debra Damo. I tried to see him Telemakos's age, serious and innocent, and could not imagine that heavy brow on a child's face. Indeed, I could not remember anything of his look other than his worried scowl. It frustrated me.

We were given a stone-built pilgrim's cottage to stay in and had supper brought to us twice. I do not know if that was a real mistake or evidence of more vigilance. No less than three young girls came by to see that we had enough water, and the old man who kept the pilgrims' cells was desperate for court gossip. He brought us a goat so that Telemakos could have milk. Then he sat outside the door of the hut until long after dark, chewing some kind of bitter-smelling leaf and plying Turunesh with endless questions about the New Palace.

"Have they replaced the lions in the lion pit?"

"Not yet."

"Ai, all of a year now has the palace at Aksum been without lions! What will become of the kingship?"

Telemakos appeared in the doorway like a wraith, his hair a halo of silver in the light of the waxing moon.

"Who said lions?" he asked.

"Go to sleep," said Turunesh.

"I cannot sleep while everyone is talking about lions."

"You will have tomorrow's great adventure all to yourself," Turunesh said. "Go to sleep."

In the morning we had another long uphill trek to reach the ascent to the monastery. But when at last we came there, we knew that Telemakos could not make the climb to the entrance by himself. The snake of leather rope that led to the portal hung nearly a hundred feet down the side of the cliff.

I had not come this far to be thwarted by a rope. I handed my bow to Turunesh and set out to take Telemakos up the amba myself.

At the foot of the cliff there were sentries, who helped visitors to fix themselves in the leather harness, and who gave them guidance as they climbed the cliff side. They, too, had the look of priests, and yet seemed to have a hard edge of strength to them, like soldiers or guardsmen.

I set my mouth in the harshest expression of severity and disdain, and stared into all their faces as though I were a king. I said nothing aloud, but indicated that I wanted to go aloft with Telemakos.

They gazed at Telemakos with a deeply interested and

intense scrutiny. I was annoyed that holy men were not better able to disguise their fascination.

"The boy?" the eldest of them asked.

"He is here to act as messenger for me," I said.

When they heard my voice, they knew I was a woman.

"You cannot stay here," the spokesman said. "You cannot touch these things; you cannot look at this place."

At once I felt my arrogance to be mean and discourteous. I knelt, and bowed my head. "Forgive me. I thought to spare the child the ascent."

They seemed unable to tear their gaze from Telemakos. They tried to answer me politely, but I could tell that their attention was greatly diverted.

"One of us will bear him for you," said the man. "What would you have him do here?"

For one moment of panic it occurred to me that I did not know for certain whether Caleb was here. It had all been implied and hinted at, but nothing had been spoken.

"The child is my messenger," I repeated. "I seek the lord of your land. I am daughter to Artos the high king of Britain, and my father is dead."

"The one you seek is here," said the sentry. "I do not know if he will see you, but the boy may take him your message."

I knelt by Telemakos and held him by the shoulders.

"Hey. Hey, Telemakos Meder. What are you going to say to the great person when you meet him?"

"I shall make a full reverence, on my face on the ground,

and say, Your Highness, Goewin the princess of Britain is here to see you, Goewin the daughter of Artos the dragon."

"And apologize for having to ask him to come down to me. But you see they will not let me come to him."

"All shall be well," Telemakos said, with an echo of his mother's calm. He smiled, but he was serious. His front teeth were finally through, and it made him look older. "Caleb will remember me."

"You are a bold hero."

I kissed him on the forehead and got to my feet.

"One of us will bring the boy down when he is finished," said the spokesman, "with any message there may be for you."

They helped Telemakos onto the back of one of the younger men, and belted them together at the waist. I watched as they ascended the cliff. Telemakos fixed his eyes on a spot at the back of the man's head, his lips pressed together, his expression fierce and determined. He looked so like Medraut.

I made my way back to Turunesh to wait. She handed me one of our saddlebags to drink from, and then stood with her arms folded, gazing with narrowed eyes toward the cleft in the cliff where the linteled gateway to the monastery was improbably set.

"Brave Telemakos," she said.

"They would not let me take him up."

"I did not think they would," Turunesh said mildly. "They were likely angered that you thought to try."

"I wish I hadn't. I felt ashamed."

We stood back and watched the cliff face in silence. We stood so long without speaking that I did not say anything aloud when at last I saw someone starting down the cliff, but reached out to grip Turunesh by the arm and pointed.

The climber bore Telemakos on his back. He seemed strong and sure-footed, though his cropped hair was white. He kept his face turned aside to Telemakos, nodding reassuringly toward the child who clung to his shoulders. I watched the man's bare feet against the rock, and the chiseled edge of his bearded cheek that I could see.

"Well, they have not sent us Caleb." Turunesh sighed.

"He is not even Aksumite," I agreed. "He is too fair."

"Perhaps they send a foreign guest who speaks your language."

And then, as the man descended nearer, I sat down hard on the valley floor, gasping as though the wind had been knocked out of me. Turunesh bent over me in concern.

"What is it? What is wrong?"

The shock so stunned me that I could not speak. The climbers had reached the cliff's foot and were unbinding their harness straps before I could shape any kind of words or speak them aloud. At last I managed to choke, "It's Medraut."

CHAPTER X

✧

Cloth of Gold

HE CAME BEFORE us, with his son bound and clinging to his back. His right hand was lifted to clasp Telemakos's small fingers over his shoulder; with the heel of his left hand he rubbed brutally at his eyes.

Telemakos threw me a look of wild hope and bewilderment. Then Turunesh, without speaking, helped to untie Telemakos and set him on the valley floor.

Medraut never let go of the small brown fingers. Telemakos sat down next to me, clutching up handfuls of grass and earth with his free hand as though he could not believe his good fortune at being on the ground again. Medraut stooped by him on one knee, and with his forefinger gently, gently tilted the child's chin up toward his own face, gazing into the smoke blue eyes with the wonder of a man seeing himself in a mirror for the first time.

Turunesh still said nothing. She stood watching her lost

lover and their son, her hands clenched at her sides, and began to sob.

"Mother, Mother!" cried Telemakos, leaping to his feet and snatching at one of her balled fists, and half pulled back by Medraut, who would not let him go.

Turunesh drew Telemakos close, but she could not stop crying.

"Why are you here? How did you come here?" I was shouting. *"Why did you leave me after Camlan?"*

Medraut turned toward me, still clinging to Telemakos, and wiped at his eyes again, and shook his head.

"He doesn't talk," said Telemakos. "The monks said he has not spoken a word since he came to them."

"Ras Meder?" said Turunesh softly, and held open her hands to him. "Medraut?" He ducked away from her touch, ashamed, unworthy.

"Why?" she asked.

He shook his head again and sat on the sand next to me, his eyes on the horizon. After a few moments he held out a tentative arm. Telemakos threw himself at his father. They bent their heads together, white gold against white gold. Turunesh gave a cry of anguish.

Medraut buried his face in Telemakos's shining hair.

"Is it true?" Telemakos said.

"Yes, love," Turunesh whispered.

"Telemakos, what happened?" I asked. "What happened when you went to find Caleb?"

"The monks brought me to Ras Meder."

I was dumbfounded.

"But I told them to take you to the emperor! I said—" I stopped short, trying to remember what I had said.

"You said lord of the land," Telemakos reminded me.

"Meder," I breathed. "Medraut. Oh, my brother, you must think we came here looking for you. But we came looking for the emperor Caleb, the negusa nagast Ella Asbeha. We did not know you were here."

Medraut nodded slowly, understanding.

"Come with us to our shelter, and we'll explain."

He sighed, and finally let go of Telemakos. Turunesh reached to help Medraut to his feet. Then she bent over his hands, pressing them together and gently kissing them, before letting them fall.

"Come, Telemakos," she said, gathering herself. "Lead on."

Telemakos, too, snatched at Medraut's hand and kissed it. Then he ran, and Medraut followed more slowly. I watched him from behind, saw how confidently he made his way down the hillside, saw how he favored the leg that had been broken at Camlan. And in his purposeful, uneven stride I recognized the silent merchant sailor who had walked away from us at Gabaza, the man Priamos had suspected to be tracking me down the Red Sea.

"Turunesh!" I said, snatching at her arm. "He was on board the ship that brought us from Alexandria. He must have—he must have followed me all the way—he must—"

He had tracked me from Camlan.

"And so he hid his hair beneath a head cloth, and never let us see his face! We thought nothing of his fair skin; there were Grecian oarsmen onboard as well. He must have come here straightaway, after we landed in Aksum. He saw me safely to the governor's house in Adulis, and went his way. My God, how did he trace us through the Mediterranean? We changed ships in Septem and Priamos arranged it that we left a day early. . . ."

I stopped, then said in wonder: "Priamos feared for me through every mile of the journey. I teased him for it. Oh, God, it is *unthinkable* he should stand accused of treachery!"

Turunesh stared after Medraut as well, as baffled as I.

"Oh, why," she whispered, "why did he not come back to me!"

Medraut never spoke, his steady silence awkward and unhappy. With Telemakos following at his heels he watered our horses and milked the goat. Then, ill fitted as it was to him, he borrowed my bow and loped off into the wilderness, his pace only a little irregular. He came back in the afternoon with a small antelope over his shoulders. I talked to him alone as he cut up the antelope. He worked quickly, efficiently, not looking at me. It felt as if I was talking to the face of a granite wall.

I told him of Priamos, and of Constantine, and finally, hesitating, of my hold over Telemakos. He put down the knife and wiped his hands on the grass. He watched me, listening, but he did not nod or shrug or raise his eyebrows or do any of the little things that people do to make themselves understood. It was as though, in forsaking speech, he forbid himself any kind of communication at all.

"Is Caleb here?" I asked.

At last Medraut gave me a single, brief nod.

"Will he talk to me?"

He shook his head. It might have meant no, it might have meant he did not know.

"Medraut," I said, trying to make my voice gentle and reasonable, as if I were talking to Telemakos, or one of Telemakos's birds. "Medraut, you owe me the favor of begging me an audience with Caleb."

He looked at me with narrowed, burning eyes. There was in his look a little of the old outrage he must have felt when Lleu used to order him about.

I could well imagine what he was thinking: You take my son hostage, then command I grant you favors?

"Do you know what you left me with after Camlan?" I demanded.

He picked up the knife and set back to his work, as if this, too, were one more guilt that he could not bear. I continued relentlessly: "You left me hunted by your heartless and vindictive mother. You left me with my father's legions and no one to lead them. You left me alone to seal and lock the iron gates on my parents' tomb. And when I did that, finally, I had to do it knowing I might be sealing those gates on you as well, alive under the earth. It was not a fair decision to leave in my hands, Medraut. It should not have been my decision. I should not have had to hold myself responsible for your death."

He gave another single, unhappy nod, jerking meat from bone with wet fingers.

"I have come in search of the emperor's head cloth, to crown his heir. I need an audience with the emperor Caleb, with Ella Asbeha. I need it as a supplicant on behalf of his son, on behalf of his nephew, on my own behalf, on your son's behalf. I know your silence is a penance; find your way around it. One diplomatic niceness from you can bring freedom for two, three, four princes."

He held his hands up. Stop, his hands said. Stop. I will do it.

That night after we had eaten, he sat before the fire outside our shelter with Telemakos in his arms, as though the child were an astonishing gift that he had never expected and could not quite believe.

Turunesh repeated suddenly, but this time out loud: "Oh, why, why did you come here, why come to Debra Damo, why did you not come back to me?"

Medraut pulled up a handful of earth from the valley floor and let the dust trickle through his spread fingers. He held his hand there open, empty, and closed his eyes.

"I ask nothing of you but yourself," Turunesh said.

I laid one of my own hands on his shoulder. He looked as though he needed steadying. Telemakos glanced up at me.

"This is all too hard," I said. "Let's sleep. Then let's share a day or so together, eating and drinking and building cooking fires, until the shock of today's meeting is behind us."

"Stay with us a day," Turunesh agreed lightly, as if she did not care whether he came or went, though her voice still shook.

Telemakos echoed, "Stay."

Medraut slept with us in the stone cabin that night. I closed my eyes to the usual mad cackle of hyenas and night birds and opened them to the sound of Medraut's voice.

He was talking in his sleep, as he has always done.

I knew his voice instantly, dark and musical and low, and full now of anguish and misery. Medraut spoke so softly he woke neither of the other sleepers. I think it must have been my own deep longing for home, for all things familiar, that made his quiet voice wake me.

He spoke, in our native British dialect, of the copper mines at Elder Field. It took me some time to work out what he was talking about, because he mumbled and muttered and did not connect his thoughts. But as I lay awake listening, fascinated and horrified, I understood how he came through the caves at Elder Field. He had not meant to find his way out. He spoke of being pressed in a narrow cleft, of thirst, pain in his pinioned leg, of running water.

I had to wake him at last, to shut him up.

He stared at me, appalled. He must have been aware he had been speaking, though perhaps not of the content of his words. He climbed heavily to his feet and left the shelter. He was back in our enclosure as the sun rose, stirring the charcoal fire before even the goatherds were away. He stayed with us for two more nights, but he did not sleep with us again.

He kept apart from Turunesh. She gazed after him with longing, as though from a distance. He never touched her.

On the third day Medraut climbed back to the hermitage and did not join us again until late in the afternoon. He carried a leather bag, and shepherded us all into the dooryard of the cottage. When he had us captive and attentive, he drew from the satchel an Aksumite head cloth. As he unfolded it, with almost reverent care, I saw that it was not the simple white cotton that everyone wore, but linen woven through with gold thread so that it sparkled like sunlight on water. The three ribbons that banded it across the forehead and tied at the back were of solid gold mesh.

It was the imperial head cloth of the negusa nagast, Caleb's own. Medraut laid open its folds, spread the cloth between his hands, and held it up to me.

"So simple as that?" I whispered.

He shook his head, once, and held up a finger. *Wait.* He unwound the shawl from about my hair and unpinned my plaits so that they hung down my back, out of his way. Then he banded the golden cloth across my forehead, and tied it behind my head. When he had finished Medraut reached again into his leather bag, and this time brought out the simple circlet of gold that had been Lleu's crown.

"Ai, my brother," I whispered.

For a long moment Medraut bent over the slender gold band balanced gently between his hands, his shoulders hunched together tightly, as though he were being whipped.

"Oh, Medraut," I said softly, "is there no way to heal you of Camlan?"

He shook his head. Then he raised the circlet to his lips and kissed it. He had failed his brother and killed his father, and there was nothing left in him for anyone else.

He looked up. He crowned me with my brother's crown and beckoned me.

"What are you doing?"

He beckoned me again, patiently. I followed him out of the hut and along the rocky path to the foot of the amba.

"I am not allowed up—" I began.

Medraut touched the circle of gold over my brow, and the head cloth beneath it. He touched my lips gently to stop me talking.

The emperor's head cloth would allow me passage.

CHAPTER XI

Debra Damo

"FIX YOUR GAZE on the portal above," the sentries advised me at the bottom of the cliff, as Medraut adjusted the leather sling around my waist.

Two dark faces waited for me at the portal, one aged and lined, one young and smooth. The men helped me onto the ledge that served as their gatehouse. I stood breathless with the view and the climb, as Telemakos must have done earlier, while I waited for Medraut to follow me.

Beyond the portal was a narrow passage of rough-cut slopes and stairs between steep walls of rock. At the summit of the tortuous climb the plateau opened to a world of its own, a city in the clouds, floating serene above the valley floor. Stone houses were scattered across the wide tableland, built in imitation of the great houses of the capital, with flat roofs and high walls enclosing them. The church there also was built of geometric blocks and tiers, and I recognized it from the *Red Sea Itinerary*.

We passed a small reservoir cut into the stone of the mountaintop, its edges green with moss. Higher up I could see the rim of another.

Here: ten years ago. Priamos and Hector were chained back to back in one of these, for giving a spear to their mad brother, Mikael. Mikael was still here, somewhere.

I walked resolutely at Medraut's side, holding my crowned head as fixedly as a face on a coin.

Medraut took me to a thatched shelter in a sunny garden, where men worked and weeded companionably. There was a strong scent of herbs and goat hanging in the thin air. By and by one of the novices brought us some of the fried cakes of which Candake was so fond, and honey with them, and honey wine.

The sun was setting when Ella Asbeha joined us.

The emperor Caleb was a small, neat man, older than my father. His hair, like his sister's, had gone white, and his beard was cropped close around his dark, lined face. He was dressed in the simple shamma of undecorated woven cloth that all the novices wore. And yet he was Aksum in all her many climates, from her salt basins to her clear and verdant highlands to her ice-capped peaks; grudging and forgiving, generous and unyielding, constant and unpredictable, all at once.

I thought, in that instant, that I was boldly presumptuous in pretending myself a queen only to trick an audience out of this imperial and holy man. God help me, what was I thinking in coming here, how would I ever come away from this beautiful and terrible place alive, with my soul and my mind and my freedom intact? I was ashamed to be sitting before Caleb wearing his borrowed head cloth, or even my brother's crown. I lay with my face in my arms.

Caleb said to me, in my mother's native dialect: "Britannia, there is no need for that. Not from you; and not here."

I rose to my knees but could not make myself stand. I was a supplicant; it seemed appropriate.

"Are all you children of Artos so full of humility?" Caleb said, again in my mother's tongue, and there was humor in his voice.

"Why did you send my father your lions?" I asked absurdly, like a sphinx posing a riddle.

Oh, he laughed and laughed, and even Medraut turned his face aside.

"Did you come from Britain to ask me this?"

I thought of Priamos's introduction to his uncle: *Solomon walks among us in your wisdom.* "Please excuse me," I muttered, trying to pull my thoughts together, still on my knees.

"I sent Artos my lions to seal our coalition," Caleb said gently. "I was not going to leave them for the viceroy Ella Amida; he has no right to them. And Wazeb will have to find his own."

Then Caleb addressed Medraut in Ethiopic. "Ras Meder, will you stay with us while Britannia tells her story?"

It was dusk now, and two of the novices came by with torches that they fixed in the ground just outside the tent. An evening wind stirred across the amba, bringing with it the sound of a single voice chanting from some unseen place on the plateau. The full moon came blazing forth as I spoke, so bright you could see colors in the dark. The torches were eclipsed.

Caleb said, when I had told him all, "So in effect you would agree to marry Constantine, if he allowed you to choose Britain's king yourself? Whom then would you choose, Britannia?"

His manner of addressing me was unnerving, but made clear the serious formality of his questions. I glanced at my brother and held open a hand toward him. "My father's eldest son still lives," I said.

"He no longer speaks, though," Caleb pointed out, and asked suddenly, "Whom would you choose, Ras Meder?"

Medraut pointed to me, and Caleb chuckled.

Then the emperor motioned one of the attendants to his side and whispered to him. The boy went running off into the molten dark.

Caleb turned back to me. "Wait a moment for the child to return," he said, "and I will show you something."

We waited. The distant clear voice continued to sing.

And then the messenger came back. His hands seemed empty, but Caleb picked something small from his open palm.

"Have you ever seen an Aksumite gold piece?" the emperor asked me.

I thought of the brave sunburst on Constantine's new coin. But that had been copper. "I don't think so."

"Here is one of mine," said Caleb, and he held out a thin, bright coin. It winked more golden than rising moonlight as he passed it across to me. Its face showed the profile of a king wearing a heavy and elaborate tiered crown.

"Is this you?"

"The image is a symbol," said Caleb, "not a close likeness. You will find a like portrait on hundreds of years of Aksumite coins. See, on the face is the king, royally robed and crowned, and here he bears the imperial fly whisk that scatters the enemy like insects. Now here—"

Caleb flipped the shining disc over on my palm. "On the reverse the king is no more than a man, the servant of the people, wearing only a head cloth."

It was a simple counterpart to the king on its face. Three ribbons banded the head cloth in place, tiny stripes across his forehead. The delicate miniature contrasted sharply with the first figure: crown, no crown; king and mortal man; image and opposite.

"A king's power may come from God, but he is not a god," said Caleb. "When you do battle against Ella Amida, Britannia, are you battling the king he represents, or the man he is? What wrong has he done as a king? Look carefully at the other side of the coin."

I sat silent as Medraut, and thought.

Constantine had arrested Priamos for abandoning a post he had, in fact, abandoned. Constantine had had Priamos punished for running riot in a palace that was held in stewardship for another, and Priamos had chosen the punishment himself. Constantine had placed a guard over me because I, a foreign princess barely past girlhood, was followed through the streets by a crowd of beggared soldiers. Constantine had found Telemakos lurking in his office and had turned him out with a slap on the head.

I stared down at the engraved face on the coin in my palm, modest in its shining head cloth, then turned it over. The crown glittered in the torchlight.

Constantine was not a kind man, but he was an excellent viceroy. I prized and valued kindness, but I knew it was not kindness that would repair my father's war-torn kingdom.

I glanced at Medraut and remembered that he, too, had had a thundering argument with Constantine before half the imperial court when they first met, whatever that had been about.

"You know Constantine better than I do," I murmured to my brother. "Would you give him your blessing as high king? Would you step down to him?"

Medraut bowed his head, then nodded once.

I laughed, a little hysterically. "Oh, God help me, I don't know what to do. You are the man who would barter your kingdom for a cup of coffee!"

Caleb laughed also. "I think you have put your threat to Ella Amida the wrong way around, Britannia. Agree to make him king only if you may choose your own husband."

The distant chanting stopped. The moon sailed high. I gazed down at the coin in my palm.

"I will make him king," I said decisively, "if Priamos goes

free and fully pardoned. Then Priamos may complete his com-mission in Britain as Constantine's ambassador, though I dread having to mediate between them."

I could not remember what Priamos looked like smiling; in my memory he wore a permanent frown. It made no difference. To speak his name made tears catch in the back of my throat.

"Priamos goes free," I repeated firmly. "And Telemakos—"

Medraut placed his lean hand over mine where I held it open on my knee, lacing his long fingers between my own and locking the gold coin between our palms.

"Telemakos is blameless," I said. "He is already free."

"Your plan has a single flaw," Caleb said.

"What flaw?"

"It leaves Wazeb with no British ambassador."

"Oh, yes," I said.

Medraut squeezed my hand. I saw that he was looking at me, a curious expression of fond admiration in his face. He let me go and softly touched the top of my head, as though he were blessing me.

I said calmly, I made myself sound as calm and serene as Turunesh: "We expected my twin brother Lleu, late prince of Britain, next in that position; so if Wazeb will accept it, I will stand in Lleu's place."

Caleb did not answer immediately. I remembered to lower my eyes, but held my head high, feeling the cloth of gold and the narrow crown weighing heavy on my hair.

"You are a child," Caleb said. "You are a woman."

I heard the paradox in his words before he did.

"There are no women allowed in Debra Damo," I answered, "yet I am here."

It was a place of paradox, Debra Damo, prison and sanctuary, a double-sided coin.

"Neither truth has ever prevented me from acting. Let me represent my kingdom in your capital as I represent it here, tonight."

Then Caleb's laughter rang across the high plateau.

"Done, Britannia."

The night air was like coffee: sharp, dark, uplifting, strong with excitement. I breathed deeply of it and bowed my head before the emperor.

"Thank you, Highness," I said. "I will serve as I am able."

The emperor Ella Asheha stood up. He beckoned me to rise also. "You will sleep here tonight," he said, "but do not remove the head cloth while you are in this place. It is only my borrowed sovereignty that allows you here, and you may not stay more than this one night. Nor should you otherwise delay your return. Priamos will be suspected in your disappearance, and will be harshly used if anyone thinks he encouraged you to peril."

I hissed sharply. How could I not have seen that? Placing me in harm's way could be punishable as real treason, punishable by death.

"And he deserves better," Caleb added, musing. "No other has been so adamant in his loyalty, or has been tested so severely. He is the best of Candake's brood."

Caleb paused, then finished lightly, "You will be given a room in the royal enclosure, where my nephews sleep. Ras Meder will show you the way. If I do not see you in the morning, Britannia, I wish you God's speed and God's blessing. I am sure you will serve both our kingdoms well."

I could not sleep in the hard, bare, beautiful house that they called the royal enclosure. I lay awake and stiff all night, in the place where Priamos had passed his childhood, afraid that I would damage Caleb's head cloth if I moved in my sleep while I wore it. In truth, there was no reason I could not have taken it off in the privacy of the room they gave me for the night; but Caleb had warned me to wear it, so I did. It felt like cloth of lead, not cloth of gold, by morning.

I saw no one in that house during the night, after Medraut left me alone. But as he led me out again in the morning, we passed three men. All three were dressed alike, in plain shammas of unbleached homespun, but the two younger men seemed to act as retainers for the third. He was my father's age, perhaps slightly younger. He talked animatedly to his companions, or to himself, waving bent and twisted hands as he spoke. He was quoting scripture, I think, glibly and at great length. His wrists were all but ruined with arthritis. I thought he must be another veteran of the Himyar.

He fell abruptly silent when he saw me, then threw himself flat on his face on the stone floor at my feet.

I was stupid with lack of sleep. I had no idea what this could mean until Medraut lightly touched the head cloth that I still wore.

"Please stand up," I said to the man at my feet, in Ethiopic.

He did, and held out his gnarled hands to me as if in supplication. With no idea of his intent, but moved by his severe deformity, I laid my hands in his. He could scarcely close his fingers around my own, but he lifted them closer to his face and stroked them as had the queen of queens, as though fascinated by them.

Then I saw that his crippled wrists were patterned with the same faint scars that marked Priamos. And though he no longer wore the chains that Priamos had spoken of, I knew that this was Mikael, Candake's mad and tragic eldest son. How long had the arthritis been eating at his wrists to make them so misshapen, and did he still demand his serpent-slaying spear? He could never hold a spear, let alone throw it.

No one spoke any word as he looked at my hands. No one told me his name, or explained to him who I was. His companions and mine all stood alert and ready to restrain him should he seem to threaten me, but he was very gentle.

At once it occurred to me that his amazement was not to do with my pale skin.

He let my hands fall at last and rubbed his eyes.

"No one tells me a thing," he said plaintively. "I hear nothing."

Then he turned and walked away, still shaking his head. His calm companions followed him.

"Why was I never told that the emperor is a woman?" he complained, and went his way.

FORGIVENESS

CHAPTER XII

✦

All the Wealth of His House

MEDRAUT NEVER OPENED his mouth. He was a walled city with no gates, his spirit inaccessible, unworthy of his father's kingdom, unworthy of the woman he deeply loved. But whatever other bonds he might shed like oiled cloth sheds rainwater, he could not resist Telemakos.

Medraut came back to Aksum with us. On the night of our return he wandered about Kidane's mansion like a bewildered ghost, touching fabrics and ornaments, leaning out of windows, gazing up at the carved ibex and cheetah on the coffered ceiling. Telemakos shadowed him, as he had done all through our homeward journey. He held his father's hand, or leaned insinuatingly against Medraut's waist like an affectionate cat, chattering incessantly in a low voice. It was the exact way he talked to his wooden animals. You could hear what he was saying, if you listened carefully. He was filling in the missing conversation.

"Ras Meder asks, 'What is that picture, Telemakos?'

"Well, sir, that is Menelik traveling to visit his father, Solomon. Menelik is going to steal the Ark of the Covenant from Solomon's palace when he leaves.'

"Ras Meder says, 'That's not right, is it, boy?'

"Indeed not, but Solomon will forgive him."

Or again:

"Ras Meder says, 'Look, child, can it be that this is the very lion skin I gave to your mother, before you were alive?'

"It is, sir; it has an esteemed place in this house. No one but yourself or a chieftain may wear it."

Medraut had the child underfoot almost constantly, and must have heard it all. He never answered, but I could see him biting down on rising tears, could see his jaw and hands tightening as he flinched against the assault. Telemakos would walk a far, hard road before he healed his father, but effortlessly he won his father's heart.

When we made ready for our parade to the New Palace on the following morning, Medraut appeared among us prepared for his role like a general returning triumphant from war. He had shaved clean his face and cropped his hair short, in the style of a Roman senator. Over one of Kidane's well-made shammas he wore Turunesh's lion skin. The glaring head crowned him, and the shimmering black mane hung over his shoulders and down his back. It must have been heavier than battle armor. He had no other ornament. He stood taller than any of Kidane's household; he looked like Caesar Augustus.

He gave me the only smile I had seen from him in the

weeks since we had found him: a proud, bitter smile of encouragement.

"Medraut son of Artos," I said.

He bent his head in acknowledgment.

I smiled back at him, and said with determination, "Let us go now and give away our father's kingdom."

He held out his arm to serve as my escort.

It was a triumphant march to the palace for me, accompanied by the party of priests that Caleb had sent with us to bring his blessing to Wazeb. Passersby stopped to bow and kiss their wooden or silver crosses, instead of veering away from my guard. Medraut walked into the New Palace as though it were his own. Everyone knew who he was, though it had been more than six years since he had been in the city; with Artos dead, for all anyone knew, this was the high king of Britain. I sailed in his wake, outraged at how simple this was for him, at how simple all the last year would have been for me, if I had been a man. Medraut did not even have to open his mouth.

It was a day of clear, scoring sunlight, and we found Constantine afoot in one of the training yards, watching a troop of spearmen at practice. The yard was sited so that the crenelated shadows of the palace's towers tricked the eye and made the spearmen's targets difficult to see. Rows of seven soldiers at a time took turns casting in unison, with unerring precision. I waited for Constantine to call them to a halt. He stood with seventy armed men ranked at his back, and I with my sundry entourage of priests and child and mute.

"Saints be praised, Princess, I had nearly given you up for dead!"

Constantine grasped me by the elbows in a warm yet formal embrace, and kissed me on either cheek.

Well, so he should.

"I have been frantic for your safety—" He stopped abruptly, and stared at Medraut. Then he fell to his knees.

"My lord. My king."

Constantine knelt before Medraut. He knelt, and waited to be told to rise. Medraut, of course, said nothing.

"I submit to your authority," said Constantine.

Would I were a man. Here was I to bestow on him a *kingdom*, and still he addressed my companion as though I were not there.

My voice seemed loud in my own ears as I said, "I mean to make you high king of Britain, my cousin. It pains me a little to do so, but you are my father's chosen heir. Your regency ends as Wazeb becomes the emperor Gebre Meskal, the servant of the cross. I bring Caleb's blessing for his son, and have crowns for you both."

Constantine glanced up at Medraut and said hesitantly, "My lord?"

"I have crowns for you both," I repeated, with fearful warning in my voice. "I have brought you the crown of the prince of Britain."

"My lady."

Constantine finally inclined his head in my direction.

He challenged: "Here stand a son, a daughter, and a grandson to Britain's high king. Three of you stand before me alive and whole, and still you would offer me this kingship?"

"Not without condition."

"Of course not," Constantine acknowledged bitterly, just as though we were battling in his study once again, as if he were composing a new set of choice words to tell me how stubborn and irrational I was, only he could not embarrass himself before the troop of imperial spearmen.

"Of course not," I agreed, temperate and composed. This was not a battle, and Constantine would see so eventually. I waited.

He murmured at last, "What are your conditions?"

"My engagement to you is sundered, that I may stay here in your place, as Britain's next ambassador to Aksum."

He blinked in surprise. Then I saw his jaw tighten, and knew it for jealousy, as he considered what I might do alone in Aksum after his return to Britain.

"There's more," I said, cool and proud.

"Go on," he answered politely, through his teeth.

"Ras Priamos shall be freed, and formally pardoned by you. Caleb and I have agreed that Priamos must return with you to Britain to fulfill his embassy there under your rule."

Constantine knelt quiet, nonplussed and speechless for a moment. Then hesitantly he began: "What then of your talk of choosing Britain's heir. . . ."

He glanced at Telemakos. I shook my head warningly.

Constantine gathered himself. "Who then will follow me?"

"Your issue," I said, "or your choice. You shall not be bound to me any more than I to you."

Again I waited. The terms were set.

"My lady," Constantine said, and this time turned his reverence to me as well as his words. "This is a fair and generous offer. I will serve as I am able."

Then, to one of the officers, "Bring Wazeb."

"Bring Priamos," I commanded, with cold and absolute authority, though my cheeks burned as I said it. I had not seen him since the Meskal parade. I had not spoken to him for more than two months.

So they joined the congress: Wazeb in his unadorned white shamma, emperor to be, wearing his cross of twisted grass like the novices from the monasteries or the children of the mountains; and Priamos with his two attendant spear bearers, like a pretender to the kingship.

Constantine saw it, too. He barked out, "My God, but this is madness. He has the very face of treachery."

But why, why? That heavy brow, which I had held dear and inaccurate in my mind for so long, seemed faintly worried; but not treacherous. Eyes lowered, Priamos wore the careful, blank expression that meant he was hiding himself. I knew that look. It was the look Priamos had worn as he knelt to have his hands whipped. It meant he was afraid and would not let it show.

I stamped one foot in an agony of impatience and

restraint. Here was Constantine calling Priamos before seventy armed warriors; for all Priamos knew he was being summoned to his execution. What had he endured this past month, waiting for my return, suspected of collusion in my disappearance—

"I will test him for you," said Wazeb. He came forward to stand before the practicing guards, then raised one arm above his head.

"Let fall your spears," he commanded.

The forest of spiked barbs disappeared. There was scarcely a clatter as the ranked soldiers gently placed their weapons on the ground.

"We must have a royal hunt before a royal investiture," Wazeb said. "No man becomes a king until he has proven his strength."

"A royal hunt—a lion hunt?" Constantine objected, out of habit, I think. "You have not the experience!"

"It is a ritual," said Wazeb, mildly. "I have never heard of a king killed in a royal hunt. What do you think the spear bearers are for? I shall choose mine carefully. . . ."

His tranquil, imperial gaze fell on Medraut.

"Take Nafas's spear, Ras Meder," said Wazeb evenly, "and aim at the third target."

Constantine's ceremonial guard passed his lance to my brother.

Medraut is an archer. He had not held a spear in close to a year, and it was not his weapon of choice; but I have never known him to miss a target. He did not hesitate, now, but neither did he make any kind of haste. He weighed and test-ed this unfamiliar weapon for a long time, finding its balance, measuring his mark. When at last he let the spear fly, he threw heavily, without the fluid ease of the trained soldiers. But his aim was as true as any of their best.

"So," said Wazeb, "that is one reliable spear behind me."

Medraut took a step forward, as though he would speak, and moved a hand in protest.

"Only for the hunt," said Wazeb. "It is a favor. There is no obligation attached."

It was more than a favor; it was a tremendous honor. The lion skin Medraut wore snarled sightlessly at us as Medraut bowed his head and closed the fluttering hand.

"Ras Priamos," said Wazeb, "take the other spear."

I saw Priamos's shoulders rise and fall, as though he had breathed a quick sigh. He seemed to frown, but it might have meant nothing. He did not look at me. But his step, the swing of his body as he moved clear of his guards, was so easy, so eager, so suddenly without tension. Constantine's second spear bearer casually passed his weapon to Priamos, and Priamos stood holding it impassively, waiting for the next command.

"The fifth target," said Wazeb.

Priamos did not weigh the spear. He scarcely took aim. He threw almost blindly, in sheer freedom of release.

His cast went wide, and he laughed.

Wazeb said lightly, "You are out of practice. Throw again. Use Tedla's lance."

Tedla was one of the guards over Priamos himself. Tedla did not simply hand over his spear: he bowed his head and knelt before Priamos, offering up the lance as if in ceremonial tribute.

"Thank you, faithful one," said Priamos. "I am indebted to you, now."

"Never," said Tedla. "I and half the soldiers in this city would not have come home from the Himyar without your intervention."

"I did nothing. There was no act of wit or courage on my part that brought us home alive and free. It was Abreha's generosity."

"Take my lance, Ras Priamos," said the soldier.

Priamos did so, without another word, and threw again at the fifth target. And as he did I noticed things I had never seen in him or thought about before: how he lifted his spear with as much effortless grace as did the negus's guards; the smooth glide of limb and torso as he launched the spear, the force with which it struck his mark; and the way he folded his hands slowly shut at his sides as he came to attention again, nodding slightly as he judged his cast. How could I not have seen how easily and fluently he moved, or that Caleb had trained his body as thoroughly as he had trained his mind? How could I have ignored or forgotten such whole and complete beauty in favor of one single striking feature of his face, in favor of his accidental frown?

"Better," said Wazeb. "Now throw again, so we are sure it was no accident. The seventh target."

There was only one spear still raised, not on the ground or stuck fast in a bale of straw, and that was held by Priamos's other guard. As Priamos took it from him, I saw what Wazeb had done: he had seen to it that now Priamos alone was armed, of all the assembled throng of soldiers. If Priamos had intended revenge or treachery, it could have been his in that moment. He could have killed Constantine, or Wazeb, or taken any one of us as a hostage. His sovereign lord was granting him a public display of trust and honor.

Priamos threw again, well in control of himself now, and Wazeb said at last, "Well struck."

"Well spoke," I said quietly, "Gebre Meskal; emperor of Aksum."

Telemakos lost his head. In the stillness that followed my words, he exploded into a run and hurled himself across the playing field at Priamos, crying out with open arms, "Now you can go hunting with the princess!"

Priamos lost his head as well. He swung Telemakos aloft as though the child were his own, then held him tightly to his chest and showered the silver hair with kisses.

"Have you given my brother his cup of coffee yet?" I asked Turunesh. "The one he said he'd give away his father's kingdom for?"

She smiled. "He hates coffee. He was being sentimental."

"I'm going to make him drink it." Turunesh had taught me how to perform the coffee ceremony, and it gave me a great and absurd pleasure to manage it deftly. "I've still to instruct my king and my ambassador in what they must accomplish on their return to Britain, and I've yet to see them speak directly to each other. I am sick to death of these formal meetings in the New Palace. Let me serve them coffee in your garden."

It was a week since our return from Debra Damo. All politics seemed to be swept aside in the plans for Wazeb's royal hunt, and I, with Constantine, was growing anxious over the fate of my own distant kingdom. Constantine readily accepted my invitation to coffee. He might be Britain's high king, but he suddenly found himself with no place in the Aksumite court, and that was hard for him.

"Wazeb, Gebre Meskal, is a madman," said Constantine, sitting stiffly upright in Kidane's garden court with his arms folded, watching me light Turunesh's burner.

Priamos and Kidane watched also. Medraut and Turunesh sat side by side, across from me. Except the time she had kissed his hands in greeting, I still had never seen them touch each other; but Telemakos stood between them, leaning in his casual, affectionate way against his mother's side, one small brown hand holding tightly to his father's large fair one. Medraut and Turunesh were, unquestionably, united; Telemakos linked them.

"The emperor is a madman," Constantine repeated. "He forbids me to leave until we have hunted together. I fear for Britain."

"Yes, I do as well," I said, speaking slowly as I watched the flames in Turunesh's borrowed burner. "But if we do not wait for the Red Sea winds to change, we will have an overland journey of a thousand miles, and in all honesty, I think another month will make little difference now."

"I am with Constantine," said Priamos. "The emperor is a madman."

"I am glad you have found something that you and Constantine agree on," I said, pouring steaming water over the roasted seeds. "Tell me then, what reason have you to accuse your new sovereign of madness?"

"He has invited Abreha to join the hunt," said Priamos.

I dropped and smashed the pot and spilled hot coffee all down my front, and gave a scream that was more of fear than pain. Medraut, you can imagine, came pelting across the court. Constantine leaped to his feet, shouting for an attendant, and Priamos dragged me to my own feet by one wrist.

"She has scalded herself—" he cried, and Medraut lifted me off the ground and carried me straight into the cold water of the stone pool.

I sat among the weed and fishes, gasping and choking, drenched. "It's all right, it's all right. My shamma caught most of it."

Turunesh found herself at once trying to calm Telemakos and to keep him from treading in broken pottery. Kidane bellowed for a nurse and a broom. Priamos and Constantine hovered helplessly at the pool's edge, as I and Medraut peeled back layers of fabric so that we could expose my arms and shoulders to the air, hunting discreetly for burns. "I should not have screamed so. I was frightened—"

There was a narrow band of stinging red skin arcing down

from my left shoulder. Medraut poured handfuls of water over it, hesitating to undress me further.

Priamos flung himself down on the rim of the pool, bent double with his face in his arms, shaking with sobs. "Ai, sweet lady, well am I named Hornbill! My wild speech is more treacherous than any plot! In the shared cup of a single afternoon I do you more harm than all your enemies have ever done—"

He glanced up wildly. "Ah, Goewin, Goewin, I will cut out my tongue myself if I have hurt you!"

"Priamos, I am not hurt!"

Unthinking, I reached to wipe tears from his face. Medraut pulled the soaked cotton cloth back across my shoulders.

"Goewin?" said Priamos softly.

He had never called me by my name before.

"Let me change my clothes," I said, feeling more scalded by Constantine's scorching, silent gaze than by the coffee. "Let me change my clothes, and then you may both tell me about Abreha."

I was sure they would kill each other on this confounded lion hunt.

CHAPTER XIII

✧

Arabia Felix

THE YOUNG EMPEROR'S hunting party included some four hundred courtiers and nobles, porters, cooks, and servants, as well as oddments like myself and Turunesh and Telemakos and even his nurse; I could imagine what Constantine must have thought of the expense. I could seldom come near Priamos, nor Medraut, who were at Wazeb's back as the negus's spear bearers. And Constantine dogged me, as though he found it necessary to take over the job of his foot soldiers now that they had been dismissed.

We traveled south from Aksum and descended into the gorge cut by the Takeze River, a northward-flowing tributary to the Nile. We followed the Takeze toward its source, until we came to a wide plain at the foot of the Simien Mountains. It was not far from Aksum, but the grassland and forest seemed empty after the cultivated fields surrounding the city. Late in the afternoon on the second day in this high valley,

Wazeb took it into his head to set those of us who were on horseback at racing.

"Whatever are they doing?" I asked, as the emperor's retinue taunted and chased one another. It was a chill and sunlit evening in December, the air sage-scented and colored like liquid gold.

"It is guks," said Turunesh. "A game."

"It's a royal game of Tig," Constantine said.

When one rider came close to another he would hurl a wand at him, which the other would duck, or fend off with his shield.

"I see Wazeb isn't playing," I remarked.

"Oh, he is. Gebre Meskal is the puppeteer. He guides the strings," Constantine explained. "He will not compromise anyone's loyalty in a personal challenge."

Now Wazeb said a word to Priamos, who turned on Ityopis.

"Come on, you skulking minister of dinner parties! You soft-pawed mongoose of a man! When did you last spur your horse to a gallop? Can any mount still carry you after so many years of your mother's fried cakes? Has anyone ever seen you race?"

"*Hai!*"

With a yell of outrage, Ityopis snatched a blunt spear from one of the footmen and tore after his brother, laughing. Their shouts were muffled by the thunder of hooves.

"So, Constantine," I said. "Are you playing?"

Constantine shrugged. "I have no great skill at this."

It is beneath your dignity, I thought, but restrained myself. There was no reason to nettle him.

"It's Medraut who's not playing," said Turunesh. "No one dares challenge him. He did once unseat three riders in an afternoon."

She added, not without pride, "They are all afraid of him."

"Well, I'm not afraid of him," I said scornfully.

Then I was seized with the kind of deviltry that used sometimes to overcome Lleu. Medraut was such a self-contained prig; somebody had to challenge him. I neither knew nor cared what rules of protocol I might be breaking: this was my brother, my lifelong friend and opponent.

"Ras Meder, Medraut son of Artos, you posturing stiff-necked hermit!" I cried. "We used to call you marksman! How long has it been since you rode in the hunt? You'll never catch me!" I crouched down in my saddle and tore away.

God, it was good to race. I glanced over my shoulder and saw, with a thrill of excitement and crazy joy, that Medraut was pounding after me.

We left Wazeb and his band on the river's edge. Medraut could not get close to me. I slowed my horse and came to a halt, waiting for him.

He was smiling. His mouth had quirked unaware into its odd, characteristic half-smile, amused and relaxed. Since before Camlan, I think, I had only ever seen the ghost of that smile, in Telemakos.

Medraut reached over to give me a playful clout on the

shoulder. I laughed. Then he raised his head, scanning the highland fields.

"What is it?" I asked.

Medraut pointed at a dark and glinting patch that moved across the plain beyond us. It would have had the look of an approaching herd of buffalo or gazelle, but for the glitter and toss of something like gold in its midst.

"It looks like a hunting party."

Medraut nodded, narrowing his eyes and gazing into the distance.

"It is Abreha," I said.

Medraut saluted me, then turned quickly and rode back toward our own party. His first duty now was as Wazeb's spear bearer.

With fearful speed, our huntsmen became courtiers and soldiers. The racing contestants now waited in ordered ranks, bright with armor and ceremonial silks, as Abreha's embassy approached. Medraut and Priamos stood opposite each other in place at Wazeb's shoulders, each armed formally, and somewhat vainly, with a short spear cast in solid gold.

"Well," Constantine remarked, at my own side, "At least Priamos makes a show of loyalty."

It was outrageous, I laughed aloud.

"Priamos Anbessa is the most loyal man I know. Let him serve you faithfully, and he will. What does everyone see in him that makes him such a monster?"

"We see Abreha," answered Constantine simply.

"Abreha, still chewing over the evils of Abreha! Heaven

help us! We are all awaiting Abreha's great offer of reconciliation," I said. "What has Priamos to do with it?"

Abreha's company had landed at the southern port of Deire and trekked across the Salt Desert, a more arduous journey than our own. They marched solemnly with pennants and silken fringes fluttering. I could hear nothing but the whine of insects and the distant squeal and titter of baboons as we waited for the Himyarites to join us.

Priamos stood frowning ferociously. Like Ityopis, he had covered his hair with a head cloth bound with silver to mark his nobility. I thought of the image on the reverse of Caleb's coin.

I looked toward Abreha's arriving retinue and saw, crowned and frowning, the coin's opposite face.

I thought I must be hallucinating. I glanced back at Priamos, and then again at the approaching suzerain who must be Abreha. It was no trick of the light. They were form and opposite, reflections of each other. They were made in each other's image.

It was not his kinship with Abreha that made everyone distrust Priamos so; it was not his tenuous alliance with Abreha after the battle that ended the war in Himyar. It was his face.

Priamos looks like Abreha: he must be like Abreha.

Abreha's party drew near and came to a halt before us. Abreha dismounted and gave his reins to an attendant. He even moved like Priamos; he walked with the same lanky grace. When he came before Wazeb and slowly lay down on his chest in a profound reverence at the young emperor's feet, it was with the same sincere courtesy that Priamos affected, when he was being courteous.

"You may kneel," said Wazeb, and Abreha rose to his knees. Priamos stood tense at Wazeb's back, glaring as though he disapproved of the whole expedition.

"Gebre Meskal," said Abreha, "Your Highness, I am your servant. I would like to offer you a formal tribute from the state of Himyar, to be granted annually, in return for recognition of our independence."

"In what name do you offer this?"

"In my own," said Abreha, "as najashi, that is the Arabic for negus; as najashi over Himyar, Saba, Hadramawt, and over all their Arabs of the Coastal Plain and the Highlands."

"I accept your fealty," said Wazeb, "and will not insist on those lands being named in my title."

The blade of Medraut's spear caught a glancing ray of the fading sunlight as he shifted his grip on the shaft. I tore my gaze from Abreha to look at Medraut, and saw that despite his blank expression his face was a river of tears.

There was no adder, as there had been at Camlan. The kings would treat in fair exchange, the warriors could hang up their shields. There would be no battle.

"I have already sent a shipment of myrrh to Adulis in anticipation of this agreement," said Abreha. "We have had an abundant year."

"Your harvests are ever abundant," said Wazeb. "What is it the Romans say? Ras Priamos, remind me of the old Roman name for the Himyar."

"Arabia Felix," Priamos answered faintly. "Arabia in fertility, O prosperous Arabia."

"O fortunate Arabia," said Abreha.

"Princess Goewin," Abreha said to me in Latin, "I would like a British representative in Sana, our capital."

I sat alone in the evening, close to the camp fires; Turunesh was singing good night to Telemakos. Abreha knelt before me and kissed my hand.

"May I sit with you?" he said, and I moved aside to make room for him on the carpet. He sat down, cross-legged. A young servant handed goblets to each of us and poured honey wine from an earthen flask.

"Wait," Abreha said, and put out a hand to stop me drinking. He sipped his wine before I did, in formal courtesy, as though he were tasting it for poison. He let the warning hand fall then, and raised his cup to me.

"Your health and good fortune."

He tilted his head to avoid meeting my eyes, as Priamos did, as though they were identical clay mannequins cast from a single mold, one a bit more worn than the other.

"I am agog to hear of the war in Himyar from the man who ended it," I said. "All who marched with Priamos speak reverently of your mercy."

"I do not think of myself as merciful," Abreha said. "I have fought too many battles and killed too many men, and will again if driven to it."

Even their voices were alike.

Abreha turned and handed his drink to the cup bearer, and placed his hands on his knees. He sat there, still and at ease, and I could almost believe it was Priamos waiting for me to speak.

"I do not understand," I said slowly, "why Caleb did not inspire the same loyalty in you as he did in Priamos. He trained you as his translator, did he not? What difference was there in his treatment of you?"

"My loyalty lies with Himyar," Abreha said, "not with any man."

"I understand that. But how did your loyalty change?"

"I cannot speak for Priamos," Abreha answered quietly. "I became the man I am because I saw what Caleb did to Mikael, my father's eldest son."

His voice fell so low that I could barely hear him.

"Mikael was younger than Gebre Meskal is now when the command came for him to be put in chains like a bond servant at auction. I was no bigger than that bright fox kit of your brother's get. I could remember no life before being sequestered; my brother Mikael was mother and father to me. After a week in irons Mikael had dislocated both his wrists, struggling to break free of the fetters. But even while they tried to mend him they kept him bound above the elbows."

I had seen those crippled, twisted hands.

"Why was it done?" I whispered.

"He had tried to escape Debra Damo. He was Candake's eldest son, rival to Caleb's sons by lineage. No other reason that I know."

Abreha coughed, and turned his face away. "Pah, I cannot speak of Mikael. It makes me sick to think of him."

He stared at the flames.

"Mother of God, how I have hated being made to war against my brothers! The day our father died, Caleb began pulling his nephews out of imprisonment and training them to send against me. Hector was murdered before I ever met him. His mutinous officers imagined I would thank them for it."

Abreha reached for his cup again.

"The men that slew Hector I sent back to Aksum. Caleb may have punished them himself. I would not accept their fealty, though they pledged to serve me."

I did not mean to judge him. But I heard myself ask coldly, "How did you bring yourself to put Priamos in chains when you took him in battle?"

Abreha swirled his wine in its cup, gazing down into its depths, and for some while did not answer. Then he said seriously, "Let me tell you, Princess, what I saw when my young brother was brought before me, stripped and bruised and bound, after a pointless slaughter of young life that he had initiated in Caleb's name."

Abreha looked up, but his gaze was still directed at the fire and not at me.

"I saw myself."

I murmured, "You are very like."

"I did not know who he was, Princess. My first thought was that it must be some kind of sorcery. You cannot imagine. He had not slept for two days; he had just learned how his dearest companion had been betrayed and murdered; he had himself been clubbed senseless with a blunt spear at the end of his battle. And there are fifteen years between us, but when he was dragged before me it was as though I were a boy again and staring at myself in a glass. My officers had prepared him for this meeting, and he obeyed when they made him lie prostrate at my feet: naked, my arms chained behind my back—"

As though amazed at his mistake, Abreha slapped the carpet at his side so that the dust flew in the firelight. "Behind *his* back," Abreha corrected. "His arms chained behind his back.

"I saw myself, Princess," he repeated. "I saw myself on the verge of manhood and obeying my king unquestioningly, instead of doubting both his wisdom and his authority. I saw myself barely more than a boy and already utterly defeated by grief and failure, instead of expecting fulfilled ambition. I saw myself forced to lie on my face in the dust before an enemy I had no hope of besting."

Abreha drew a long breath to steady himself, as I had seen Priamos do a thousand times.

"I told him to stand up. And I covered him with my cloak. He ate with me that night and slept in my tent. He was too tired to consider that my kindness might cast him as a collaborator when he returned to Aksum."

"But you must have considered it!" I exclaimed, then sighed, and put down my cup. I bent against my knees with my head in my arms, trying to understand how this man whom I liked and admired could have used Priamos so heartlessly, when it was more than I could bear to be denied his companionship.

Abreha said, "I felt that Caleb had saved Priamos to send me at the last, to be his final, surest weapon against me."

He sipped at his wine again. "By the saints, the boy was trained as a *linguist*. 'Speak Arabic if you like,' he told me. 'You do not need to translate; I am fluent in fourteen languages.' What madman would make a general of such a one, and risk splitting open a head he had carefully crammed with fourteen languages? All I can believe is that when Caleb first saw how like me the boy was, he changed his mind about how Priamos should best serve him."

"But that is not statesmanship!" I burst out.

"Well, what is it, then?"

"Trickery, gambling, delusion, I don't know. What sheer lunacy, to wager the future of your empire on a boy's face!"

"Is it any more lunatic than to wager it on the head of your newborn infant son?" said Abreha. "Or that of your nephew? Is that not how your father chose his heirs?"

I could make no answer. I had done that, too.

"I did consider how unfavorable a light my kindness would cast over Priamos," Abreha acknowledged. "Caleb meant to use him as a weapon against me. How better to destroy a sword without breaking it, than to blunt its edge? No man in Caleb's court would trust Priamos, after the battle at al-Muza. Though Caleb did, still; he sent Priamos to Britain."

"It was not meant as exile," I interrupted, defensive of my kingdom, and of Priamos.

"Indeed not. It was an important appointment, and I think it was bitterly contested. But four thousand miles is a safe distance. As you know."

The najashi smiled. It was the same joyous, childlike smile that Priamos so rarely gave. You serpent, I thought, you are more manipulative than Caleb himself, or Medraut, or even Morgause—there was no one I knew who could so coldly and consciously exploit a young life he or she claimed to hold dear.

No one but myself, whispered my conscience, and I could not bring blame against him.

Once more Abreha handed his cup to the young servant. I saw that he carried himself with a serenity and gravity that Priamos lacked.

"I will send you an ambassador," I said. "At least, I will see to it that Constantine sends you one." I rose to my feet. "Will you excuse me now?"

He rose with me. "With pleasure. And I hope we may speak again, soon, of lighter and happier matters." He bowed his head to me and kissed my hand again.

"With pleasure," I echoed. "Good night to you, najashi, King of Himyar. May God bless your renewed alliance with Aksum."

Constantine was waiting for me beyond the firelight; he may have been lurking there all through my conversation with Abreha. He bowed and said, "If you will not come home with me as my queen, at least let me escort you to your tent."

I gave him my arm and said nothing.

"I do not understand how you choose your companions," Constantine said.

"I am Britain's ambassador," I said. "Did you not also share polite conversation with the king of Himyar, when you were in my place?"

"For these few days he has the unusual opportunity to speak directly to Britain's new high king," said Constantine, "and it is clandestine mischief to approach the ambassador first. Wazeb does well to guard his back."

"*From me?*" I hissed.

I dropped his arm. I had never known such anger.

"You dare! I have given you my *kingdom*. You dare question *my loyalty?*"

When he turned to me, I struck him in the face. He stood gaping, and I slapped him again.

"You, Constantine, you, who have done so much to heal Wazeb's kingdom for him, how can you not see what a wonder they are working, Wazeb and Abreha? There is more to politics than coinage!"

"But what risk!"

"Bother to the risk! What courage!"

We stood before the small tent that I had to myself, as befitted my station as princess of Britain. I took a deep breath and spoke calmly.

"A king need not be kind, but by my father's sword, Constantine, my cousin, he must be able to forgive. Cynric the king of the West Saxons had no desire to bring about my father's death. He wished me to marry his grandson, but he never wished me any ill. You will have to treat with him yourself before a year is out."

"What on earth do you know of forgiveness?" Constantine said bitterly, then turned on his heel and left me.

CHAPTER XIV

Swifts

I SLEPT SO late the hunt left without me. I lifted the silk covering of my tent and stepped outside; the air was bright and cool and still. Women pounded grain across the camp, and a pair of young porters crouched near them playing gebeta in the dust. How lovely, I thought, to stop being princess of Britain for a moment. I hope they stay away all day.

I found Telemakos building a city out of bones and twigs and seedpods in the grass outside his mother's tent.

"Mean things, to go without you," he said sympathetically. "Ras Meder wouldn't let them wake you. He stood in front of your tent shaking his head and waving his gold spear at them."

I laughed. "I don't mind. I was tired last night. Can I help?"

"You can lay a road. I'm digging a reservoir."

His nurse and the cooks and porters must surely have

thought me a madwoman, the princess of Britain at play in the dirt. But it was contenting work.

"When will Gebre Meskal wrestle his lion?" Telemakos asked, without looking up from his excavations.

"He is not supposed to wrestle it," I said, tipping handfuls of pebbles along the road. "He is supposed to kill it with a spear."

"He is supposed to bring back a lion to the New Palace for a totem," said Telemakos. "What use is it if he kills it?"

"More use than it would be chained in the lion pit!"

"It does not need to be chained." Telemakos straightened for a moment, and spread his hands open on his knees. "You can keep a thing without tying it up. You know."

Then he shook his head and went back to digging in the earth with a pottery dish.

"Anyway, the emperor had better get going. He missed another chance yesterday, as well as last week. There were three lionesses and twice that many cubs chewing over a zebra in the rocks behind the spring, the last place we camped."

The gravel slipped from my palms. I sat back on my heels and stared at my nephew's shining head, bent in concentration over his miniature reservoir. "Where did you hear that?" I asked.

"I did not hear it," Telemakos said with scorn and pride, still without looking up from his work. "I found them myself. I watched them all through the noontide, while everyone was napping. They were lazy, too. It would have been an easy fight.

"Noon is the best time for exploring," he added. "Everyone else is too idle to chase you, and the animals are all asleep. You should come with me."

"We are going to have to put a guard over him," I told his nurse.

Wazeb killed his lion that morning. The hunters came striding back before noon, giddy and triumphant, with Wazeb borne aloft on their shoulders, his customary white blood-stained in their midst. Telemakos was not so wildly disappointed to have missed the grand occasion as I expected him to be; he was scornful of the killing.

I took his advice and went riding in the heat of that day. I had gone no more than three hundred yards beyond the perimeter of our camp when Priamos caught up with me.

"Peace to you, my princess."

"You've been lost," I answered, and found I was biting back tears, again, again. I looked away from him. "How do you come to be released from your post?"

"Gebre Meskal has dismissed me for the afternoon. It has been a trying morning, and he thinks I need to rest."

His horse seemed skittish, and he had constantly to gentle it and whisper to it as we spoke. The short spear he carried against a sudden meeting with lion or leopard became a hindrance.

"Tell me of the hunt," I said. "Was Wazeb heroic?"

"He did seem fearless, yes. He is fearless. Though so

should I be with Ras Meder at my right hand. Sometimes I think your brother has ice running in his veins."

"Sometimes I think so, too," I said impatiently. "Tell me what happened!"

"We drove a lone male lion for something close to twenty miles before Gebre Meskal wounded him. And then our new emperor had to finish it on foot, face to face with fang and claw. Oh, your brother, I have never seen him happier."

"I am sorry to have missed it."

Priamos managed to control his mount at last, and we rode some way farther. Before long we found ourselves surrounded by a herd of bushbuck antelope. They moved with us at a leisurely and steady pace, so that they seemed to be escorting us. The females were plain, but the males were deep black with slashes of white at their throats, and crowned with spiral horns.

"You cannot go anywhere without a following of vagrants," Priamos said to me.

He wore the drawn look of exhaustion that I had seen in him after Camlan and during the tribunal. I reached to touch his sleeve, in sympathy, and he glanced at me with a quick look almost of fear—as though he were surrounded by tyrants and expected blows from anyone who came near him.

"You do look tired," I said. "You look like you are under interrogation."

He smiled ruefully. "That is nothing to do with the hunting. I did not imagine I should ever have to face Abreha's lieutenants again." He sighed. "Tharan, the older man with the handsome mustache, had charge of me before I was brought to Abreha at al-Muza. I am embarrassed to think what he remembers of me."

"Abreha told me you bore yourself with great dignity."

"I do not remember anything like dignity. I fought like a bull elephant when they bound me, and vomited over Tharan's feet when it was finished. He told me I had blinded a man in one eye with the end of a chain, fighting them, but I do not remember it."

I closed my eyes and swallowed hard.

Priamos said unhappily, "I should not tell you such things. I am sorry."

"I wish you had told me more six months ago! I wish I could bear some of your blows for you!"

"Never."

"Always!"

He, too, bit his lip, as though he were my mirror. We looked away from each other.

I shook my head angrily. "I wish you had told me about Abreha. If I had known how like you are, I would have understood the bala heg's inordinate fear of you."

"I did tell you."

"So, you said you were alike, but I did not take it to mean you might well be identical twins!"

"I am not Abreha," Priamos answered patiently.

"So I know," I said. "So I know. You are Priamos."

I glanced sideways at his sharp, frowning profile, and it made me ache in heart and body.

"It is very silly to judge a man by his face," Priamos said defensively.

"I don't."

"That is true," he agreed, and gave a real smile at last. "You do not."

He added, "Neither did Caleb."

Then I knew why Priamos had served him so faithfully, despite all Caleb's contradictions.

"Neither does Gebre Meskal," I said.

The bushbuck left us, and my horse fell prey to her companion's nervousness, so we turned back. We could see men stirring in the camp when we drew near again. Abreha himself met us, also on horseback.

"Be warned, Princess," he said, half in jest and half serious. "You run a great risk in making such escapes from the emperor's protection."

"I did not go far," I said. "And I have my bow."

Priamos said apologetically, "Well, but he is right. It is outside the bound of protocol. You are not riding with your brother or fleeing a death sentence. You are representing your kingdom in a ceremonial pageant, and I am an inappropriate companion."

"A true and brave companion," I contradicted. My horse startled, as though in great fear, and it was all I could do to stay seated and calm her.

Abreha dismounted and took his own horse by the head, softly coaxing the trembling animal. Priamos bent low over his saddle to whisper in the ear of his mount and came so near to being thrown that he dropped his spear. He looked frowning over his shoulder at me.

"What is the matter with these horses?"

Mine danced in a nervous circle, fighting her reins, and I saw what startled them so.

Telemakos came toward us out of the bush. He carried a lion cub over each shoulder, two large, squirming, glorious bundles of tawny golden fur spotted with fawn.

"Idiot child," Abreha scolded, "don't carry them like that, the teeth so close to your face!"

We three were no more able to aid Telemakos than if we had had our hands tied to our terrified horses.

"Put them down," I ordered.

"I will not!" Telemakos said. "These are for the emperor."

I hesitated, then let my horse have her way. She ran headlong toward the camp, I dragging her back as much as I dared, so that I was able to slide from the saddle once we were safe within the circle of tents. Constantine caught me.

"Lady!"

"Let go of me! Bring Medraut!" I shook him off. "Where is Medraut? Tell him to take a spear and run southeast of here—"

I had Medraut and Constantine, both carrying spears, on either side of me as we raced back on foot toward the place where I had left Telemakos. I gasped out what was happening as we ran.

"Only approach quietly," I managed to say. "The horses are frantic."

"There's a lioness about," Constantine guessed briefly.

Abreha, Priamos, and Telemakos were exactly as I had left them. Priamos had managed to dismount also, but neither he nor Abreha could do anything with the frightened horses. Telemakos also had his hands full, and his path blocked. He looked very cross.

"Which way have you come?" I asked him. "Where was the lair?"

"It is only a little distance," Telemakos said angrily, his slate blue eyes gone smoky and cold. "You need not all make such a fuss. They are a gift for the emperor. I would not let them hurt me."

Oh—fearless, as in my dreams.

The great, golden kits writhed and swarmed over his shoulders, struggling to break free. Telemakos held them as firmly as he held Candake's cats, and with as little regard for the strength of their claws.

Medraut laid down his spear and knelt to look into his son's eyes. Whatever Telemakos saw there was so fearsome that he burst into tears.

"Do not kill them," he begged. "I will let them go, if I must, but don't kill them. I was only trying to bless the kingship."

"You mad thing!" I exclaimed, half inclined to laugh.

"What of their mother? She will come hunting for them! What if she had caught you alone?"

Medraut saw the real danger first. He snatched for the spear that lay at his side, and stumbled to gain his feet. The knee that he had broken earlier that year collapsed beneath him; he missed the spear and missed his footing. In the moment before the lioness was upon us, he cried out in a terrible voice, "'Ware Telemakos!"

One of the brothers Anbessa threw himself at the child. They went down together in a flash of gold and dark limbs. I could not tell whether it was Priamos or Abreha.

My bow was in my hand unbidden, and I set arrow upon arrow in the lion's throat. I shot as Medraut shoots, coldly, accurately; but my bow was not strong enough to kill her outright. The man who had flung his body over Telemakos lay crouched with his narrow hands locked behind his neck, in the desperate hope that if he were attacked he would lose only his hands and not his life. The lioness stood over the man and the child for a fragment of a second, bewildered by the stinging arrows in her throat, scenting the kits.

Then Constantine gave a great cry of fear and anger, and lifted his spear and caught the snarling creature through her breastbone. I shot another arrow into her throat, so close to her now that the shaft buried itself to the fletching. Between spear thrust and arrow's point we took her at last, between us, Constantine and I.

Constantine worked his spear out of the heavy, golden carcass and stood panting, stunned, his hands smeared with blood. The rest of us flung ourselves at the cowering man and boy. I should say the cowering man, for the child was not in the least cowed. He still clung to his lion cubs as though he would never let them go. They had torn his shirt to ribbons. Medraut, moving with his own recovered leonine stealth and speed, plucked the cubs from Telemakos's hands by the backs of their necks. The great cats went limp, as kittens do when carried so. They were enormous kittens.

It was Priamos, of course Priamos, who had chanced being rent to pieces in defense of my nephew. The cubs had torn long scratches across his face, traveling from the bridge of his nose over his cheek and down his throat. Abreha let the horses go, now that the danger was past, and crouched at his brother's side searching for any more serious injury. I snatched Telemakos close against me, and he wound beguiling arms about my neck.

"Can I keep them? I mean, can we keep them? May I present them to the emperor?"

Medraut stood helplessly holding a lion cub at arm's length in either hand. Constantine rubbed one hand against his sandy forehead and left a great red streak there.

"Well, so it was you," he said wearily to Priamos. "I wondered which of you could be so selfless."

"You did not know—" said Priamos, and stopped. Then his flyaway hornbill's tongue, and perhaps the shock of expecting the perilous teeth to close on the back of his neck, overrode all reason or gratitude in him.

"You did not know! You did not know who you were

defending! If you had known it was me, you wouldn't have done anything! You did not know, you did not care!"

"By God, I did not care!" cried Constantine. "Why, it was either you or the Himyarite king! How should I stand by and watch either one of you have your throat torn out?"

Priamos rose to his knees, shaking off Abreha's concerned touch. He offered Constantine his open hand, as though holding something precious and invisible in its cup. His pale palm was still faintly striped with the marks of the beating he had taken in the season just past.

"My lord. My king," he breathed. "Forgive me. I owe you my life and my allegiance." He closed his eyes. "I beg your forgiveness."

Constantine paused, looking down at the ambassador's bowed head and open hand.

"You shall have mine when I have yours," he said then, and took his rival's hand.

He raised Priamos to his feet. They stood firm in their shared grip, gazing down at their clasped hands, pale and dark.

"You are welcome to our coalition," Priamos said at last.

Constantine looked over his shoulder at me, and smiled.

"You noble pair of predators," I cried, in high spirit. "You are both welcome to my pride."

"Look, Gebre Meskal is coming," said Telemakos, and struggled free of my embrace.

Abreha took one of the cubs from Medraut. In the

exchange, as they both stood smiling with their heads bent over the young lions, I saw all that Medraut might have been.

Telemakos stood his ground before them, desperate. "Please, *please* don't let them go. Let me present them to the emperor, oh, *please*, sir."

He was all that Medraut might yet be.

Medraut nodded once to Telemakos. Abreha said to the child, "Stay calm and wait."

Telemakos did so. He loped at Medraut's side with his mouth pressed shut, occasionally glancing over at the lion cubs and breaking into his secretive, incomplete smile, but mostly focused on the meeting with the young emperor. When our parties came together, he knelt before Gebre Meskal with princely dignity, his impossible hair gleaming bright as any crown, and said, "Your Highness, I offer you these gifts to grace your palace as a symbol of your kingship."

Then he was on his feet, dragging forward by the elbow first Medraut, and then Abreha. They held forth the cubs.

"I have named them Solomon and Sheba," Telemakos proclaimed regally.

He held out his arms to Medraut in great longing; and Medraut, all the ice in his veins melting at this entreaty, gave him the cub. Telemakos held it cradled as if it were a house cat and offered it to the young emperor.

"This one is Sheba," he said. "Keep them well. You must not chain them."

"I will not, Lij Telemakos," said the tame lion.

❖ ❖ ❖

"Kind thought," said Priamos, as we watched them construct a hutch for the cubs to be carried in. "It was a kind thought."

Priamos had endured a thorough treatment with salt and spirits to clean the scratches on his face, which undoubtedly had been more painful than the getting of them. Now he had taken a skin of honey wine and some few minutes to regain his composure, and we stood at the camp's edge as the life of the royal hunt went on about us: the silken tents and pennants hanging still, no breath of wind stirring in the golden heat of the silent noon; the lion and lioness carried in to be skinned; Turunesh sitting before her tent with Medraut and Telemakos at her feet as her son told her of his adventure.

"We will never share a kingdom," Priamos said, his voice quiet and unhappy. "I will be in Britain before the short rains, and you still here."

"It is only for two years. I will return you your *Red Sea Itinerary* so you may find your way back. Constantine must look to his life if he fails my trust."

"He will not fail. Your kingdom will be safe in his care."

"I was thinking of my heart," I said, "which will also be in his care."

"My lady . . ."

Priamos sighed, and turned his face away from me, unable to continue.

"I understand now," I said, speaking slowly, "how Telemakos might have come to be."

"The world does not need another Telemakos," said Priamos, with equal care. "But I understand it also."

He raised his head to look toward the Simien Mountains. The sky above the junipers was spattered with a mass of swooping, screaming birds.

I stood amazed. I spoke in Latin, because I did not know the Ethiopic words I needed. "Are they swifts? They sound like swifts."

Priamos answered me in Latin. "Yes. They are not here all year. They come with the summer, and fly north before the rains."

"In Britain, too, they come with the summer. They have flown here just as I have."

"And without even an *Itinerary* to guide them." Priamos laughed. His light, sweet laughter made my throat ache. "Ai, these poor lion kits! It is like sending them to Debra Damo. There are no flights of swifts tamed and clipped and kept in cages. But how else can you keep a lion in your house?"

And because he was speaking Latin, he used the word *leo* for lion. It brought Lleu to my mind so vividly that I caught my breath in a sob as sharp as a cough.

"What is it?"

"Leo," I said. "Ah, Priamos, I have lost my best companion, and I am desolate to think that I must lose you now as well."

He did not answer. The swifts wheeled overhead, crying their high and strange familiar song.

And then Priamos did what he had never done before: he

raised his eyes to mine. They were so dark that they reflected the sky, making them seem the deep indigo-sheened coffee color of swifts' wings. I no longer saw his heavy frown, his torn face. In his eyes I saw himself, his whole being.

"Oh, my dear Goewin," Priamos said quietly, and took me by both hands. He lifted them and pressed his forehead against them, his shoulders shaking, bound by protocol against drawing me any closer than that or touching me in any more familiar way.

It was more than I could bear. I pulled his hands to my lips and kissed them gently, as Turunesh had done to Medraut. Still clutching each other's hands, we touched our faces cheek to cheek, and stood so close a moment. I kissed the tracery of a tear across his cheekbone. And then we let each other go.

Priamos looked up into the sky again. He was not frowning. His expression was caught between sudden joy and inconsolable longing.

"Ah, summer has come, and I must fly from here and into the teeth of your British winter."

Then he turned back to me with his rare, sweet, child's smile. "Do you direct the swifts northward in a little while, that I may remember you."

"And next year return them to me again."

"When they come back a second time I shall be with them."

I promised, "I shall wait."

Historical Note

✦

THROUGHOUT THE WRITING of this book, I was haunted by modern events occurring in the ancient world of my creation. In Yemen, the modern day Himyar, British citizens were being tried for treachery as I wrote. As I first set out to describe Goewin's arrival in Aksum, the modern inheritors of the Aksumite civilization, Eritrea and Ethiopia, were engaged in a bitter and bloody border war that lasted two and a half years. Each morning I would check the CNN and BBC Web sites to discover which Eritrean airports or reservoirs the Ethiopians were boasting of having knocked out that day, and how many Ethiopian soldiers the Eritreans were boasting of having killed. I was so deeply immersed in my own story of civil war and brotherly rivalry that the faces of the nameless soldiers in the photographs seemed like people I knew, Priamos's army locked in angry conflict against that of Abreha.

My retelling of the conflict in Himyar is, to all intents and purposes, based on what little fact is known about that time, even to the detail that Abreha may well have been a member of Caleb's family. I was tempted, as I learned more about the

Eritrean conflict, to model Aksum on Eritrea's capital Asmara. But I decided against it. How the Eritreans waged their successful war of independence with a handful of stolen weapons and a guerrilla army of determined men, women, and children is a story in its own right (told movingly by Thomas Keneally, the author of *Schindler's List*, in his novel *Towards Asmara*). But Aksum is Ethiopia's story, too. I did not want to take sides.

I am proud, and rightfully so, I think, of how much historical fact I have woven into this story. But my portrayal of Debra Damo needs a disclaimer: *This is a work of fiction. Any resemblance to any person, living or dead, is a coincidence.* Debra Damo is still a living, breathing, working monastery, and it is a sacred place. It is inconceivable that anyone there today would do any of the things Priamos claims to have suffered during his childhood. Yet the privations he describes would not be unheard of in Ethiopia in ancient times, and Debra Damo may indeed have been the place where the male relations of the Aksumite kings were exiled. (It is less likely that Goewin would have been allowed to visit.) The hermitage at Debra Damo was probably not more than half a century old at the time of Goewin's story; most of the origination tales for it are set in the sixth century. I have cheated in pretending it is a little older.

I have no knowledge of the ancient language Ge'ez (Ethiopic), the forerunner of modern Amharic and Tigrinya. I have used both simplified Ge'ez and modern Amharic words in this text. They are all transliterated, and in my research I rarely found the same word spelled the same way twice. I have there-

fore erred for the reader's sake, standardizing the words I have
used. In a similar vein, I have used the terms Ethiopic and
Ethiopian where it would be more accurate to say Ge'ez and
Abyssinian, for the sake of consistency and to make it easier for
the reader. Wherever possible I have tried to use Ge'ez,
Aksumite, or Greek names for the Aksumite characters
(inscriptions on Aksumite coins appear in both Ge'ez and
Greek, for Greek was the common language of the Red Sea),
but a few modern Ethiopian names have slipped in. Kidane
and Turunesh both have modern names; they were first named
in my novel *The Winter Prince*, before I had done any serious
research on Aksum, and I thought that continuity was more
important than accuracy in their cases.

Most of my Aksumite nobility have real Aksumite names,
and many of them have historical counterparts. Candake (it is
more accurately Kandake, or Candace) is not a name but the
title of the queens of the ancient kingdom of Kush; one of these
is claimed by the Ethiopians to have been their own queen.
Abreha was real, as were Caleb (Kaleb) and Wazeb. Medr, the
Aksumite deity who gives Medraut his Ethiopic name, may
have had feminine rather than masculine aspects.

Priamos is not originally Ethiopian. He has a counterpart
from Arthurian literature (as do Medraut, Llen, and
Constantine; Goewin herself is the only British character who
doesn't). Priamos appears in Thomas Malory's *La Morte
d'Arthur* as Priamus (the Romanticized spelling of his Greek
name). The son of an African prince, Priamus is a warrior who

battles against Sir Gawaine, wounds and then heals him, is converted to Christianity by him, and is eventually knighted by Arthur as one of the company of the Round Table.

Constantine, the son of Cador the Duke of Cornwall, is the traditional heir to Arthur's kingdom (coincidentally, he is named by Malory as Arthur's heir in the same episode in which Priamus appears). Among the various muddy inscriptions and unreliable legends that surround Caleb's succession, one possibility is that he appointed a regent; another is that his successor was called Konstantinos (in Greek). Obviously I have made a wild leap in making Constantine into Caleb's viceroy, but the contemporary existence (dubious though it is) of British Constantine and Aksumite Konstantinos was too delightful a coincidence to pass up.

I have taken other liberties as well. I have simplified and adjusted the Aksumite succession. My depiction of "the tomb of the false door" is a composite of several Aksumite excavations, including the tombs known as the Mausoleum and Nefas Mawcha. Coffee originated in Ethiopia, but was probably not drunk as such before the thirteenth century. (It was eaten crushed and mixed with butter in Ethiopia and the Yemen long before that, and still is; it was also made into wine—the mind boggles. Aksumite excavations have turned up vessels shaped much like the modern Ethiopian coffeepot, and there is no reason not to imagine that this highly developed civilization had not discovered the joys of caffeine.) I have stretched out the Himyar chronology a bit to accommodate the youth of some of my invented actors. The changes in titulature effected by Wazeb and Abreha are not technically accurate as represented here, but they are accurate in terms of import. After all, this is fiction, not history. Although, should anyone question an alliance between ancient Britons and ancient Ethiopians as too improbable to bother with, they might try to explain to me how a sixth-century Aksumite coin came to be found near Hastings in southern England, and why it so closely resembles the silver pennies of the eighth-century British king Offa.

While I don't want to burden a fiction reader with the ten-page bibliography I acquired during the course of my research, I would like to acknowledge Stuart Munro-Hay's *Aksum: An African Civilisation of Late Antiquity* (Edinburgh University Press, 1991; it is also available electronically at users.vnet.net/alight/aksum/mhak1.html), without which this novel could not have been written. Munro-Hay's work is, among other things, a delight to read, and a model example of a good history. I would also like to thank Jane Kurtz, who guided me past a few cultural inaccuracies; Betty Heron, who generously provided me with child-free mornings for six months; Kate Adams, who found out the answers to my disturbing medical queries; and the Whitaker family: Roger, who first told me about Aksum nearly fifteen years ago, when I asked him if he knew of a "sixth-century Christian north African or middle-eastern civilization"; Susan, for her reminiscences of the senses; Susan and Roger both, for their "Ethiopian slides" (infamous in my family for thirty years); and Rachel, for information about shipboard life, obscure genetical queries, and, probably longer ago than she remembers, the initial suggestion that Goewin's mother be able to "do something interesting, like make maps."

Elizabeth Wein
Perth, Scotland
10 July 2002

Character List

✦

IN BRITAIN:

THE HIGH KING'S FAMILY:

ARTOS: High king of Britain, father of Medraut, Goewin, and Lleu; brother of Morgause; married to Ginevra. Killed in the battle of Camlan.

MEDRAUT (called Meder in Aksum): Illegitimate and eldest son of Artos; half-brother of Goewin and Lleu; father of Telemakos. Morgause, Artos's sister, is Medraut's mother. He is the former British ambassador to Aksum.

GOEWIN: Daughter of Artos and Ginevra; twin sister of Lleu.

LLEU: Prince of Britain, son of Artos and Ginevra; twin brother of Goewin.

MORGAUSE: Queen of the Orcades, sister of Artos; mother of Medraut; Goewin's aunt.

OTHER BRITISH CHARACTERS:

CONSTANTINE (called Ella Amida in his role as Aksum's viceroy): Son of the king of Dumnonia. Artos's heir in the event of his sons' deaths; Goewin's fiancé and cousin. British ambassador to Aksum and later Aksum's viceroy.

CYNRIC: King of the West Saxons who leads a force against Artos at Camlan.

CAIUS: Artos's steward at Camlan.

IN AKSUM:

THE IMPERIAL FAMILY:

The emperor and his sons (in birth order):

CALEB: Also called Ella Asbeha. Emperor of Aksum, father of Aryat and Wazeb; brother of Candake.

ARYAT: Eldest son of Caleb, killed by Abreha in Himyar.

WAZEB: Also called Gebre Meskal. Caleb's son and crown prince of Aksum.

The queen of queens and her sons (in birth order):

CANDAKE: Negeshta nagashtat, queen of queens; sister of the emperor Caleb; mother of Mikael, Abreha, Priamos, etc.; wife of Anbessa.

MIKAEL: Eldest son of Candake and Anbessa; brother of

Priamos; nephew of Caleb. Madman sequestered in hermitage
at Debra Damo.

ABREHA: Elected king of Himyar; second son of Anbessa
and Candake.

HECTOR: Third son of Anbessa and Candake; nephew of
Caleb; brother of Priamos. Led force against Abreha in Himyar.
Murdered by mutinous officers.

PRIAMOS ANBESSA: Fourth son of Anbessa and
Candake; nephew of Caleb. Aksumite ambassador to Britain,
trained as afa negus (Aksumite imperial translator); led final
defeated force against Abreha in Himyar.

ITYOPIS: Youngest member of the bala heg (the emperor's
parliament); Priamos's younger brother; son to Candake and
Anbessa; nephew of Caleb; called "Dove" or "Peacemaker."

YARED: Youngest son of Candake and Anbessa; youngest
brother of Priamos. Musician sequestered on Debra Damo.

THE FAMILY OF THE HOUSE OF NEBIR:

KIDANE: Father of Turunesh; grandfather of Telemakos.
Host to Medraut and Goewin in Aksum. Member of the bala
heg (the emperor's parliament).

TURUNESH: Kidane's daughter; Telemakos's mother;
Medraut's lover; Goewin's friend.

TELEMAKOS MEDER: Son of Medraut and Turunesh; grandson to Kidane and Artos.

Other members of the imperial court:

HALEN: Afa negus (Aksumite imperial translator); Priamos's former tutor.

DANAEL: Aksumite minister, leader of the bala heg (the emperor's parliament).

ZOSKALES: Eldest member of the bala heg (the emperor's parliament).

EBANA: Guard over Priamos.

TEDLA: Guard over Priamos.

NAFAS: Spear bearer to Constantine, in his role as Aksum's viceroy.

Other Aksumite characters:

GEDAR: Merchant who lives in the villa across the street from Kidane.

FEREM: Kidane's butler.

Glossary

✧

G = Ge'ez, or ancient Ethiopic
A = Amharic, or modern Ethiopian
AR = Arabic

ABUNA (A): Bishop.

AFA NEGUS (G): Imperial translator (literally "mouth of the king").

AMBA (A): Mountain plateau, like a mesa.

ANBESSA (G, A): Lion.

BALA HEG (G): Parliament of advisors to the emperor.

GEBETA (A): Ethiopian game of cups and beans (similar to the more familiar African game mancala).

GUKS (A): Contest of skill similar to jousting.

INJERA (A): Flat bread made from tef, Ethiopian grain.

LIJ (A): Title for a young prince (similar to European "childe").

MESKAL (G, A): Feast of the Cross (literally "cross"), religious holiday taking place at the end of September.

NEBIR (A): Leopard.

NEGESHTA NAGASHTAT (G): Queen of queens (here, the emperor's sister).

NEGESHTA NAGAST (G): Queen of kings (title rarely given; Cleopatra is referred to this way).

NEGUS (G, A): King.

NEGUSA NAGAST (G): Emperor (literally "king of kings").

NAJASHI (AR): King.

RAS (A): Title for a duke or prince.

SANTARAJ (A): Ethiopian chess.

SHAMMA (A): Cotton shawl worn over clothes by men and women.

There is no word for "slave" in Ge'ez.

**The next installment in Elizabeth E. Wein's
masterful Arthurian/Aksumite cycle**

THE
SUNBIRD

Telemakos is the grandson of two remarkable men: Kidane,
member of the parliament in the African kingdom of Aksum, and Artos, the fallen High King of Britain. Telemakos
is also a remarkable listener and tracker, resolute and inven-
tive in his ability to learn and retain information—and keep
it secret. Now Goewin, the British ambassador to Aksum,
needs his skill. There are rumors of plague in the cities close
to the capital. Telemakos must travel to the outlying cities
where salt—the currency of sixth-century Africa—is mined,
and discover who has been traitor to the crown, ignoring the
emperor's command and spreading plague with the salt from
port to port. This challenge will take all of Telemakos's skill,
strength, and courage—because otherwise it will cost him
his life.

I

THE SALT TRADERS

Ready Telemachus took her up at once.
The Odyssey, *1:267–68*

TELEMAKOS WAS HIDING in the New Palace. He lay among the palms at the edge of the big fountain in the Golden Court. The marble lip of the fountain's rim just cleared the top of his head, and the imported soil beneath his chest was warm and moist. He was comfortable. He could move about easily behind the plants, for the sound of the fountains hid any noise he might make. Telemakos was watching his aunt.

She, Goewin, ought rightfully to be queen of Britain, queen of kings in her own land. Everyone said this. But she had chosen to send her cousin, Constantine, home to Britain as its high king, and she had taken his place here in African Aksum as Britain's ambassador. Goewin was young, barely a dozen years older than Telemakos himself. She often held informal audiences in unofficial places, like the Golden

Court. She said she liked the sound of the fountains. Telemakos sometimes lay in his hiding place for hours, listening, listening. He did not understand all he heard, nor did he talk about it. But he loved to listen.

These men were not taking his aunt seriously, Telemakos could tell. They were talking about the salt trade. One of them was an official from Deire, in the far south beyond the Salt Desert, and one was a merchant, and one was a chieftain from Afar, where the valuable amole salt blocks were cut. The men were supposed to be negotiating a way of sending a regular salt shipment to Britain in exchange for tin and wool. But their conversation had deteriorated into a litany of complaints, and they spoke to one another without acknowledging Goewin's presence, as if she were a servant or an interpreter. If they did acknowledge her, it was to make some condescending explanation, as though she were a child.

Telemakos knew how this felt. It was one reason he had become adept at keeping himself hidden. People taunted him for his British father's hair, or they touched it superstitiously as if it would bring them luck; it was so fair as to be nearly white, incongruously framing a fine-drawn Aksumite face the color of coffee. And everyone hated his stony blue eyes, for which he could not blame them. "Foreign One" was the least offensive name they gave him. It was something Telemakos had lived with all his life, and he thought he did not mind it. But it was not something to which his aunt was accustomed, and he knew that it made her angry.

She dismissed the party of merchants and officials. They

were listening with enough of an ear to her that they heard her dismissal.

Goewin sat for a moment in the quiet court then, empty of all life except the bright fish that darted through the water around the fountain. She drew a long breath, not so much a sigh as the noise she might have made before steeling herself to tease out a splinter of glass lodged in the palm of her hand. Then she said suddenly, "Telemakos, come here."

He had never been found out before, by anyone.

He was so surprised that for a long moment he did not move or answer her, expecting her command to have been a mistake, or believing himself to be dreaming.

"Telemakos," Goewin said, in a voice of dreadful imperial frost that brooked no argument, "I will not be disobeyed by you."

Telemakos crawled out from among the palms, silently, and knelt before his aunt with his head bowed.

"Do you make some use of your practiced espionage," she said. "Follow that party of dissembling tricksters and see if you can discover what tiresome plot they were hiding from me so carefully."

"Lady?" Telemakos asked tentatively, not sure that she could be serious, or why she was not angry with him.

"Follow them," said Goewin, "and listen."

So he did.

He stalked them like a leopard through the halls of the palace, gauging their attention, and watching the interaction of their servants even more closely than he watched the men themselves. They had a large number of attendants among them, from porters carrying sample bars of salt to children looking after exotic pets. The Deire official had a huge black cat on a lead. It was muzzled, and the merchant's clutch of half a dozen tiny monkeys were making it crazy. A tall boy with a thin moustache hung on to the cat's lead; four boys of about Telemakos's age seemed to be in charge of the miniature monkeys.

Telemakos, their shadow behind benches and pillars and potted trees, could not hear what they were saying. He needed to be with the party to hear them. Before he could frighten himself with the possible consequences, he slung a pebble at the leg of one of the monkeys.

He did not like to do it. But he did not trust people to react as predictably as animals. He would rather have dealt with the cat than the monkey, but there were four boys of varying shades and ages in the monkey retinue, and only the one older boy in charge of the cat. Telemakos needed to pass unnoticed.

His marksman father had never managed to sharpen Telemakos's aim, and it took Telemakos three quick shots before he struck his mark. Then there was a little explosion of temper and chaos as the monkey whirled and screamed and tried to bite back, striking out at the unfortunate child who held its lead. Telemakos ran up to the monkey, caught it by the scruff of its neck, and shook it. He gentled it while running with the other boys, who were all leaping to still the eruption and not draw attention to themselves from their masters. Telemakos stepped aside so that it looked to the monkey band as though he had momentarily crossed over from the cat band, and the haughty cat boy paid him no attention because Telemakos was obviously with the monkeys.

There was a moment, then, when he realized with a thrill through the pit of his stomach as though he were swooping from the boundary wall to the roof of his grandfather's stables, that he was standing in plain sight of twenty people and no one saw him.

The worst that could happen was that he would be chased off or reported to his grandfather, Kidane, who sat on the emperor's council. And his grandfather would not punish him. He would scold him, perhaps, but he would assume that Telemakos had been attracted to the cat, which was almost true. The roaring in Telemakos's head quieted, and he began to listen.

They spoke in Greek, and Telemakos could understand it, because it was the common language of the Red Sea. At least, he could understand the words they said, but he doubted their meaning. The men did not trust one another, and Telemakos's Greek was imperfect. He paid as much attention as he could to the sound of the words, so that he could repeat them accurately.

Cutting himself away from the group was even simpler than joining it had been. The owner of the fabulous cat suddenly turned around and snapped at his animal keeper in an incomprehensible language: "Go feed that creature!" or more likely, "Get that stinking feline away from us!"—the big cat smelled very strongly of big cat, and must have been intolerable when it was in heat. The thin moustache headed off in a different direction, pulling the cat with him. Telemakos peeled away from the party with the cat, and left its haughty keeper before he bothered to look down his long nose at the strange boy trotting at his heels.

Telemakos hugged himself into a granite alcove and stood still there for a moment, breathing lightly and trying to calm the roaring that had surged again in his ears. With most of his mind he dutifully repeated the words he needed to recite to his aunt; but with a small, delighted portion of himself he whispered aloud his new talent:

"I am invisible."

"Are you sure that is what he said?"

Goewin did not doubt that Telemakos was repeating to her what he thought he had heard. But she doubted that he could have heard it.

"'Plague will raise the price of salt,'" repeated Telemakos.

"There is no plague."

"That is what the Afar said. And the official from Deire—Anako?—Anako said that it had spread from Asia along the trade routes into Egypt, and across Europe as far as Britain and Byzantium to east and west, and that no one cared to buy cloth or spice or grain in any Mediterranean port, but wine and salt were dearly sought and dearly bought."

Goewin drew Telemakos down to sit by her on the fountain's rim.

"And what more did you hear?" she asked slowly.

"Alexandria . . . Alexandria? Where the abuna, the bishop, comes from. Alexandria is considering a—a curfew? They used a different word, but I think that is what they meant. No ships allowed in or out. And the merchant said that if there were such a law passed, it would make no difference to the African and Asian traders on the Red Sea, because they would take their goods to Arsinoë and sell them there for a dearer price. It wasn't curfew—"

"It was quarantine," said Goewin. "Quarantine."

She put an arm around his shoulders and hugged him against her. "You are a bold hero. I have told you that before."

He longed to look into her face, so pale and foreign and stern, but it would have been rude. Goewin sometimes commanded him to look at her, when she wanted his attention, but he did not dare to do it without her permission.

"Go on, then." Goewin tilted her head in the direction of the Golden Court's portal. "Go lose yourself. I've got another meeting in a minute, and I don't need you lurking at my feet."

Telemakos wandered through the busy halls of the New Palace and out to the lion pit. The emperor's lions were dozing in the shade of the young pencil cedars. Telemakos climbed down the keeper's rope.

"Hey, hey, hey, Sheba, you big bully. Get away from my feet."

Telemakos landed lightly in the grass at the foot of the pit. Sheba, the lioness, buffeted her great golden head against his; Solomon, the magnificent black-maned lion, yawned and did not move from his spot beneath the trees.

"La, my lovely, I'm glad to see you, too." Telemakos buried his face in Sheba's sun-heated fur. She smelled like frankincense. "What have you been rolling in, you pampered creature? What a waste of good spice!"

The lions' bodies belonged to the emperor, but their hearts belonged to Telemakos. He had captured them himself, as kits, and given them as a coronation gift to Wazeb, now the emperor Gebre Meskal, negusa nagast, the king of kings of the Aksumite peoples. By day they lived in the lion pit of the New Palace. They wandered freely over the grounds at night, too fat and lazy to bother the pet elephant and giraffe that wandered there also, but daunting enough to any would-be thief or assassin. Telemakos was no more in awe of them now than he had been when he plucked them, small and golden-spotted and squirming, from the nest of rocks where their aunties had left them while they went hunting.

He liked to play with the lions when his mind was empty, and to snuggle with them in the sun when he had something to think about.

Plague in Britain was what he was thinking about now. He had never been to Britain, but he felt connected to it, living daily with his British aunt. Telemakos shared Goewin's rejoicing when packets arrived from Ras Priamos, the emperor's cousin, Aksum's ambassador to Britain. It was four years since they had seen each other, but Goewin's heart was in her homeland with the Aksumite envoy, Telemakos knew; he knew how she treasured Priamos's letters, how devotedly she answered them. If plague was in Britain, Priamos might be lost to her; and if plague was in Britain, Telemakos was sure his father would never take him there.

But if it had spread through Egypt already, then might it not end in Aksum itself, and who would then waste time worrying about distant Britain?

Goewin will tell the emperor, Telemakos thought, if I know Goewin. She'll tell him this afternoon, because there's a meeting of the bala heg this afternoon; that's why Grandfather came up to the New Palace this morning. He never comes up here unless the council is meeting.

Lying in the sun with his face against Sheba's spicy fur, Telemakos conceived an intrigue so elaborate it verged on folly.

He contrived to gain entry to that afternoon's meeting of the bala heg, the parliament of twelve nobles who gave private counsel to the young emperor Gebre Meskal. Telemakos hid himself in plain sight, just as he had done with the salt traders. This time he made Grandfather believe that he was attending the council as Goewin's unlikely companion, and he made her believe that he was there with Grandfather.

Telemakos walked between them as they entered the council room, his head held high, his eyes on the floor. He could sense Kidane and Goewin glaring at each other accusingly, not daring to start a personal argument in the emperor's presence. Telemakos kept his gaze trained on the floor. He bowed to the emperor with Kidane and Goewin, lower than either of them because he was younger and had no place here. He lay on his chest on the floor with his face in his arms until

Gebre Meskal acknowledged him.

"Lij Telemakos."

That sobered him. It was very rare that anyone called him by his title, which was something equivalent to "young prince." Telemakos's mother and grandfather only ever introduced him as Telemakos Meder, his own name and his father's Aksumite name. Yet his mother was a noble and his father a prince, and though Telemakos was Aksumite by birth, by blood he had more claim to the British kingship than did Constantine, Britain's high king.

For one uncertain moment Telemakos feared the emperor would ask why he was there. Then Gebre Meskal said, as though in warning, "All right, Telemakos," speaking in tones of dismissal.

Telemakos stood up, his eyes still trained on the floor. He moved to stand aside with his face to the wall, to show how well he knew his place; he was sure that this was a courtesy Grandfather would have required of him if he had truly brought him to this meeting.

Gebre Meskal acknowledged his councilors with no more of a greeting than he had given to Telemakos, and called for their silence.

"Princess." Gebre Meskal was always as respectful to Goewin as he was to anyone, and it was partly this that kept Telemakos in awe of her. "You have news from our ambassador in Britain?"

"Thank you for allowing me entry here today, Your Majesty," Goewin said coolly. "Yes, only this noon I've received a letter from Priamos."

"I await my own," said the emperor. "The despatchers are erratic as ever."

"There may be good reason for that," said Goewin. "May I read this aloud?"

And there it was again, the evil word, *plague*. Priamos's letter confirmed that it was in Britain. Priamos apologized that he would not return to Aksum that year, as planned and expected, because he did not think it safe to travel. He also advised that Goewin stay where she was: "For to move from one land to another is to drag the pestilence from place to place, and to leave a wake of death and uncleanness in one's path."

There was a long silence after Goewin finished.

She spoke grimly, into the heavy silence, "I am going to write one more letter to Constantine the high king, and tell him to shut down Britain's ports. And I entreat you, Your Majesty, to do the same here in Aksum."

The council chamber exploded into outrage. Telemakos turned his head, very quietly and carefully, so that he could see over one shoulder a little of what was going on.

There was old Zoskales, who was deaf and always asleep, starting and blinking; his neighbor, Karkara, yelled an explanation at his ear. The warrior Hiuna and the priest Kasu, from the ancient city of Ycha, had broken into angry argument with each other; while Ityopis, the emperor's young cousin, slapped the rail before them with one open palm to try to calm them or get their attention.

Telemakos found himself shaking with bottled laughter.

Each one of the bala heg was behaving exactly as he did in court or in the street. Telemakos could not believe they were so predictable.

Goewin leaned an elbow against the rail in front of her own seat, her head tilted a little, her eyes hidden behind one hand. She waited in disgusted silence for the council to come to order. Telemakos moved his head imperceptibly, straining to get a better look, and found Goewin watching him from beneath her hand. She held his gaze for a moment before he could duck back toward the wall. His heart hammered; he was sure she had discovered him again.

Well, there was no doubt Grandfather would have him whipped this time, for this was the most outrageous thing he had ever done. But he would not give himself up until he was called out.

It was Danael who brought them to order. He was their leader, the agabe heg, the king's closest advisor.

"Have you so little regard for the British ambassador?" he thundered. "Sit down. Would you question Caleb's choice of her any more than you question his choice of Gebre Meskal as his heir? Sit down and be quiet and let her speak."

Danael turned to the negusa nagast. "Your Majesty?"

"Come to your feet, Princess Goewin, and address them again," said the emperor.

Telemakos heard her stand up. She said simply, "Close your ports. Close your borders. You will lose commerce, you will lose authority, you will lose alliances. But you have the strength to do it and survive. The world is aflame. If you would live through this scourge, you must cut yourself off from the world."

A few of the council sent up a murmur of assent. Telemakos heard Grandfather's voice among them. Zoskales muttered something, loudly but incomprehensibly, in his flat, hissing voice.

"'What is the child doing here?'" Karkara repeated clearly.

Telemakos drew in a sharp breath.

"Turn around, Telemakos," said Goewin.

He turned to face them, staring at his feet.

"I asked him here as my witness," said Goewin smoothly. "He was with me this morning when I first heard rumor of the plague, from Anako, the archon in Deire. And it was in conversation with Anako's porters that Telemakos heard speculation as to how to undermine the quarantine in Alexandria. Where there is no market, there will be a black market. So I would advise you not only to set quarantine in your own land, but also to lay careful snares against any who would slip through your net."

Now, though he was still gazing studiously at the floor, Telemakos knew they were all staring at him. The emperor said, "Tell us what was spoken, child."

Telemakos answered dutifully.

"You are speaking Ethiopic," said Gebre Meskal. "Is that what you heard?"

"They were speaking Greek," Telemakos corrected himself, and carefully repeated the salt traders' words as accurately as he could, as though he were reciting a language lesson.

"You heard this in conversation with Anako's *porters?*" questioned Karkara.

"Not exactly; it was not the porters speaking, sir," Telemakos said. "Anako and the Afar chieftain were talking to each other. I was with the porters, looking at their animals."

Another great murmur breathed through the chamber as the bala heg considered.

"When do you envision this quarantine enacted?" Gebre Meskal asked Goewin.

"Tomorrow," she said.

Tim Galland

ELIZABETH E. WEIN says: "In its original form *A Coalition of Lions* seemed to me to be deeply connected to events in Ethiopia and Eritrea, the two Horn of Africa countries that share the inheritance of ancient Aksum's artifacts, language, and culture. Their border war of the mid-90s did not receive much attention in the Western press, and I felt strongly that in writing about Aksum I was making a tiny contribution toward a greater global awareness of these struggling and beleaguered nations.

"But in my heart I am a storyteller, not a historian. After many early drafts it became clear that this book was about people, not nations: passionate, complicated, manipulative, determined individuals. In a conversation with Sharyn November, who was not yet then my editor, I was struck by a disturbing insight into Goewin's character. 'Her dark secret is that she is ready to sacrifice those she loves for the good of her country.' After that revelation, the real plot of *A Coalition of Lions* came very quickly.

"Character is plot."

ELIZABETH E. WEIN was born in New York City and grew up in England, Jamaica, and Pennsylvania. She has a B.A. from Yale and a Ph.D. from the University of Pennsylvania.

She is the author of two other books set in the Arthurian/Aksumite world: *The Winter Prince* and *The Sunbird*.

Elizabeth and her husband both ring church bells in the English style known as "change ringing." They also fly small planes. They live in Scotland with their two young children.

"ELIZABETH E. WEIN'S STORYTELLING IS RICH AND STRANGE AND WONDERFUL." —ROBIN MCKINLEY

 fter the death of virtually all of her family in the battle of Camlan, Goewin—Princess of Britain, daughter of the High King Artos—makes a desperate journey to African Aksum, to meet with Constantine, the British ambassador and her fiancé. But Aksum is undergoing political turmoil, and Goewin's relationship with its ambassador to Britain makes her position more than precarious. Caught between two countries, with the power to transform or end lives, Goewin fights to find and claim her place in a world that has suddenly, irrevocably changed. . . .

"[An] ambitious novel whose magic lies in its emotional intensity and in the unusual vibrancy and intelligence of its characters." —*Booklist*

ALSO BY ELIZABETH E. WEIN
The Winter Prince
The Sunbird

0-14-240129-3

40129>

UPC

VISIT US AT
WWW.FIREBIRDBOOKS.COM
FIREBIRD FANTASY **U.S.A. $6.99** CAN. $9.99

0 51488 00699 2

S